By
Minyetta Nelson-Bailey

THE CHAPTER THAT CHANGED MY LIFE

MOCY PUBLISHING
WWW.MOCYPUBLISHING.COM

Detroit, Michigan

Printed by CreateSpace, An Amazon.com Company

THE CHAPTER THAT CHANGED MY LIFE

ISBN 978-1-940831-31-2
Copyright © 2016 by Minyetta Nelson-Bailey

Published by Mocy Publishing, LLC.
Website: www.mocypublishing.com
Email: info@mocypublishing.com

MESSAGE TO THE READER(S)

   As a child, I thought as a child, acted as a child, talked as a child even played as a child. When I became an adult. I put away all those childish things and ways..........

This is a story about my life.   The actually story is my life. Take from it what u will. I write/type this to inform the reader(s) on my life experiences. What I saw with my own eyes, heard with my own ears and spoke with my own mouth. Things I know or knew. A lot of these details may be agreed upon then again some may be disputed but once again I inform the reader(s) that this book is from my point of view.   So if we can agree to disagree I would hope that you would continue to read and support this book.

Thank you
The Writer MInyetta Nelson-Bailey

Table of Contents

This book is dedicated to my daughter whom I am blessed to have, to experience this journey we call life with.   GOD blessed me with the love that HE knew He only could give.

The best! I love u baby.

INTRO

The story of my life begins with a name. My name.
HI! My name is Minyetta Nicole Nelson. I am a
Black African American woman with a household of
two at the moment. Consisting of my daughter and
I. I was the firstborn child to my father Rodney
Nelson of Detroit, Michigan so he wanted me to
carry his last name and I am the second born child
but first daughter to my mother. Born to Marisca
Pendarvis in the early morning of July 23rd, 1986 at
Hutzel Women's Hospital of Detroit, Michigan. At
the time of this printing in the year 2015 I am 28
years of age.

It is quoted that the decade of the 80's, "Is the
decade that made us."   On National Geographic's
website under "Explore the 80's- The Decade that
Made Us"- it reads……

"It's like totally tubular. The 80's- Isn't about
nostalgia. It's about the history of our modern
world that spawned political, technological, cultural

and social revolutions that begin in the United States and went on to dominate the world. The cultural programming event is the defining biography of a generation. It is about a decade of people, decisions, and inventions that changed our future, told from the persective of the unknowing history makers who lived these iconic moment."

My Childhood Was Not Ideal

In the peak of the summer of 1986 on July 23rd, a
beautiful baby girl was born to a mother at the
young age of 20, whom already had a baby boy of a
year old. Even though the young mother had
children it didn't slow her strut. She continued
bout her life as she had done previous to the
children. She ran the streets doing what she
wanted, living as she pleased. Being a busy body
kept the young mother busy for sure and away from
her children.   Leaving the kids sometimes in the
care of her older brother even going as far as
leaving the kids alone at times. All the while the
young mother was out living it up in the streets she
left her baby girl vulnerable and susceptible to being
molested at a very young age by her uncle.   Incest.
Committed by a family member.   Before baby girl
was even old enough to form the words to speak or
even attend school her innocence was taken.
Mind, body, soul even peace of mind violated.
Mentality and trusting ability broken and destroyed.

The young mother is not, was not around enough or long enough or maybe she simply didn't care or have that attachment to her children to know that something was going on. That her child wasn't the same. Every time the young mother chose to leave she left her baby girl with a disability. Baby girl couldn't defend herself. So she was violated again up until the day the molestation was caught in the act by another family member. The family member ran off to find the young mother a few blocks over to tell her what she had just encountered. Informing her to call the police. The uncle was arrested and convicted of CSC of a minor. CSC is criminal sexual conduct. After trial he was found guilty and sentenced to prison for some years. Even this tragic incident didn't seem to slow the stroll of the young mother. She continued bout her ways.

Now with no babysitter the young mother had no choice but to leave the kids alone by themselves. Just to be out in the streets. At home alone for some times hours. Then the hours turned into a day which eventually turned into days. I remember one time she had been gone so long that we had eaten all the food out the fridge so I had to climb upon the countertop to the check the cabinets for food. I remember having to change the baby's soiled diapers. I remember watching television all day and night waiting up for her to come home but she never came. This one time we lived upstairs in a two family flat and the downstairs neighbor would come upstairs to check on us to make sure we had something to eat. We knew it was the neighbor by the way she knocked on the door to let us know it was her. We knew when momma was home because she didn't have to knock. She had a key.

Then one day there wasn't a knock but loud bang at the door and it turned out to be the police. They gathered us up to take us down to the 12th Precinct on West Seven Mile and Woodward where Child Protective Services on Michigan were contacted to come pick us up. When the State of Michigan took over they terminated our biological mother's parental rights for lack of participation in the programs that were required of her to get her kids back. So we were deemed wards of the state. Six of us in all. Three of us, the five year old, the two year old and the one year old were claimed and placed with their father's and or father's side of the family. Leaving the unclaimed four year old, three year old and newborn to go through the process of being placed in foster care.

The first family I was placed with I was placed by myself. It was an elderly African American couple named the Coopers. They lived in a nice house in a nice area. I was too young to remember the street because I couldn't read but I did remember the numeral digits because they involved my birthday. I was with the Coopers long enough to celebrate one of my birthdays with them. I remember the Coopers throwing me a birthday party where they invited their friends and family. There were no kids but we did have cake and ice cream. I wasn't with them too much longer after that. I believe they gave me back because of their age. Me being too young with lots of energy they knew they wouldn't be able to keep up with me. One thing I will not forget about the Coopers is that they loved beans. It had to be their favorite dish or something because they had beans every day. All day. Every night. Sometimes all the time. Beans and it didn't matter what kind either. Beans were always on the menu.

My next family I was placed with would bring my siblings and I back together where we would be adopted into their family. This amazing woman whom adopted us we would call grandma only with her permission. She had already raised five grown boys so along with us her family consist now of seven boys and one girl. The daughter she never had. It didn't take that long for the family to blend and within a year or so she was going through the process to adopt us. Our case worker was an older man named Mr. Thorton. He was a well dressed and well groomed man. He dressed in three piece suits with the matching tie, hat and handkerchief with his long casual elf shoes. Elf shoes because they were so long that they curled up at the toe. Very nice and presentable man. Mr. Thorton would arrange the meetings between our biological mother and our new family. The young mother would make it to some of the meetings to visit with her kids but showed no progress in advancing to better herself in order to change the situation for her kids to increase her chances of getting them back. So the kids were adopted. They endured the process of learning one another and growing on each other.

The new environment, as a child I would find it hard to understand how and why I/we were not good enough to make our mother want to change for us, I found it uncomfortable being raised in a house full of strangers. No blood relatives. It was very challenging mentally as a child but especially emotionally. I often found myself daydreaming or wondering about my mother. It always started off with good vibes but ended up in turmoil. Good questions to demanding answers. I needed to know! I wanted to know. Only answers that she could give. Straight from the horse's mouth. I could not understand. I was lost. Totally deranged in the mind as to why she wasn't here with me, with us.   Raising us.

What was she looking for or had found that was more important to her than her very own kids? What was consuming her time away from us? Where was she?   As a child I could not make sense of these things and wondered why no one was talking.   My adopted mother tried to comfort me and ease my worries but to no avail.   The answers she gave only left me with more questions. Eventually she would grant me permission to venture out to have contact with her.   To get to know her.   To learn her so that I could learn and know myself.   The many times we met up at the foster care facility only deepen my curiosity of this lady because of the way she portrayed herself to have some type of concern for us, her children and our well-being.   Our mother would tell us that she was taking care of business and doing whatever she had to do to get us back home.   This is what inspired me to want to get to know her and believe that she wanted us back.

After being adopted, all hope was lost. I knew it was over. We had our last names changed to solidify our position in our adopted family. It still didn't keep me from wanting to know my old family just because we had a new one. By the time I began to spend time with my biological mother, it was in her own element. Her own environment. She had already started on her own new family with two baby girls and now was living with the kids father. I wasn't bothered by the fact that she had a new family, I was just excited to be in her presence. I would do everything required of me at home to leave for the weekend or school break to go over to her house. Instead of her spending time with me she was more consumed with being under her kid's father locked up in the room or hanging in the streets. Leaving us kids unattended once again and now that we were older, able to wonder the streets. So every chance I got I followed right behind my brother.

In the neighborhood where they lived he was well known and well liked. People admired him and commended him for being a young boy with a grown man personality to go along with his grown man responsibilities, which was taking care of and supporting his family.

If You Don't Work

When I started venturing over to my biological mother's house on the weekends and or school breaks I was reintroduced to my older brother. The more time I spent with my older brother the closer we became. We were all kids but my older brother had the attitude of a grown man, the mind of a hustler and carried himself as such. Running the streets, conducting business, making money, making sure he had and his family ate. Being the oldest as well as a male my older brother took it upon himself to be the "Man of the house" even though there was already a grown man in the household. That grown man did not provide like my brother was providing. The only thing that man gave out on the regular basis was ass whoopings to my biological mother. She received them almost as a reminder of who really was in charge.

My brother knew what he wanted and knew what he had to do to get it. He had a family that he had to produce for every day. Not only did he go to school every day, he also had a job as a stocker and bag boy position at the neighborhood grocery store on Harper and Seminole called Kit Kat along with posting on the corner. My brother was a hustler and he got it-the money- by any means. As a child growing up I had heard the term hustler and even had some hustlers on my biological side of the family. Everybody on my adopted side worked the usual nine to five to support their families. Running behind my brother had me feeling like I wanted to be a hustler too.

Now everything is not for everybody and everybody don't do the same things but I feel like everything and everybody can be a hustle or hustled. You just have to choose your game. Learn it. Master it and play it to the best of your knowledge , ability and always play to win. So with that being said everything I practice I learned and mastered before I even tried it. Now as a child you don't fully quite understand as well as you would if u were an adult so I sat back and watched what was going on around me with tunnel vision. Able to zoom in and ask questions at any moment. I observe people and their actions. How they go about their day, how they treat others even some of the decisions that they make. I had two examples in my life that were different on so many levels of life.

Whatever he was doing on the block didn't interfere with him being at home and or going to school because our mom didn't know. But he was doing what he felt he needed to do to help his family survive. He brought home groceries as well as money. He took care of the house as well as everyone plus himself. Treating himself to the latest pair of shoes, an outfit or just something so simple as a movie. My brother also had a flock of females that ranged from his age on up. He loved the older women because they were more stable than the younger chicks who were still living at home with their parents. The older chicks had their life together and planned. They had jobs with their own houses and cars. They would shower my brother with gifts and money. They would let him drive their cars. But none of that would keep my brother from the block. I learned everything I know about hustling the streets from my brother. The everyday combat. The hand to hand. Who wanted it and where to get it from.

Now the woman I was raised by, my adopted mother was the one who taught me about this game called life and trust she taught that game very well. From the time I laid my eyes upon her I could tell she was about her business. The way she conducted herself was very classy and upscale. Carrying herself with the utmost self –respect. I idealized her without even knowing that I was doing so. I compared everybody to her and she always came out the winner. I respected her as a person, a mother and a woman. She did something that was/is very admirable in my eyes. She chose to take three kids into her house, into her home. Her heart, to raise as her own children. Standing ovation! She took care of my siblings and I hand over foot even after raising her own kids to grown men.

She made sure that we always had, that we never lacked what was necessary in the benefits to help us grow and prosper. Always pushing us out the door to school and motivating us to do our best to get good grades with a little encouraging words, the belt and an ass whooping. That true southern hospitality. True to the grain. Through and through. We always had a roof over our head with food in the fridge and clothes on our back. We lacked of nothing and our adopted mother made sure of that. She provided a stable home and environment and brought us up with a good foundation.

Our adopted mother was born and raised in the south. Named after the state she was conceived and born in. Georgia. Married, had two of her boys while still in Georgia then relocated to Detroit, Michigan where she would conceive the last three of the five children. Later expanding her family from six to nine with the addition of my two brothers and myself. Her greatest attribute is that no matter what was going on she was always dedicated to her family as well as to herself. My older brother and my adopted mother helped prepare and train me for the rounds that I would stand in the ring to defeat this thing we call a struggle.

At the age of ten I still questioned everything. After being molested as a child by two different people, once in the care of my biological mother and the second time being in the care of my adopted mother. These incidents happened at two different stages in my life and it seemed as if no one cared enough about me to even help me, talk to me or get me out of the situation. It stunted my growth and hindered me emotionally as well as mentally. I was discombobulated. Mind all over the place and all fucked up. Especially with no counseling or anyone to talk to about what had happen to me or what I was going through. I felt helpless so I looked more toward the streets than being home. Trouble was at home.

Now with a fucked up mindset and little to none trusting ability at the age of ten I was introduced to the guy who would later become my child's father by my mother. He was thirteen at the time and was rumored to already have fathered a child with another female. We became very good friends and that's what made me open up to him about my life but he didn't seem to care about my past. He didn't judge me or act funny afterwards. He just wanted me to know that he had my back reguardless. This made us grow even more closer to each other. Over the next few years our friendship would eventually grow into a relationship and every time I would go over to my mother's house my boyfriend would come to visit and even stay the night with me.

By the Spring of 2000, I was getting ready to graduate from Joy Middle School which was located at Fairview and East Warren. I was graduating valedictorian of my class and ranked in the top five. Everybody was so proud of me with words but didn't follow through with actions. Only two people showed up to my ceremony. My mother's mother being my grandmother and my cousin on my adopted side of the family where I resided during the last two semesters of my eighth grade year. I was doing great, staying out of trouble and doing all that was required of me and more but no one seemed to care. I thought that I was doing something right. Not because I was supposed to but because I also enjoyed learning. Now that graduation was done and school was over I was now an official high schooler. It was now the summer time. I was ready to enjoy the pleasantness and all it had to offer me. Plus the summer contained the most important day of the year and it was approaching very fast. My birthday! I was excited! My vacation all planned out or so I thought.

Some Things Cannot Be Changed

The plan was to spend the majority of the break at my mother's house, where I could be free to do as I pleased and spend as much time with my boyfriend as possible. I also wanted to be able to tread behind my brother with no hassle so I could continue to learn and pick up on some of the skills of the trade. The way I had my summer break set up in my head and the way it actually happened are two different stories. The summer started off like every other summer. I was back and forth between houses, from my home to my mother's house. When I was home bound I was a good girl in all aspects of the concept. Doing as I was told when I was told with no talk back. No attitude, no hard breathing or stomping of the feet. My adopted mother did not play when it came down to kids. She really didn't play games when it came down to the respect level of any and everybody. She commanded it and honestly it was well deserved.

She watched over and took care of all whom lived in her household from the adults down to the kids. She always recommended that we play by her rules or be prepared for the fall out, backlash and ass kickings that was followed by not just her but your parents as well when it came to the kids. Some days we were confined to the house and could not go outside. Not because we were bad or disobedient but because there wouldn't be an adult out there to watch over us. When she chose to attend to us while we were outside we could only go as far as her eyes could see us without her turning to look for or call us without yelling. So we could only go as far as our neighbor's driveway.

For me being the only girl/female being raised around nothing but men and boys I had to take a liking to the things that the boys liked and what they did because none of them would want to play dollhouse or dress up with me I believed. The boys would all gather in front of the house to play basketball and or football while I played two square with one of the younger kids from down the street.

Always winning because of the way I would spike the ball downward. Eventually I grew tired of defeating my only opponent and only friend at the time so I joined in the mayhem in the middle of the street with the boys. They were playing the game of twenty one with elimination because it was so many of them. Tall, small, skinny, fat, medium and even nicely maintained boys who practiced and played for whatever school they went to. So it was a game! When I walked in the middle of the street everybody paused, looked at me and began to laugh. Not really wasting a moment of their time because the competition was so intense amongst them that they continued the game after their big group laugh.

When the ball went back out I posted up on the boy who had the ball. He looked at me, snickered to himself and as everybody watched he brushed right pass me fast like the wind. I didn't see anything! All I heard was the sound of a whistle. By the time I realized what had happened I turned around just in time to see everybody standing around to watch my opponent score a lay up. In my mind I was pissed because all the people playing were just standing around and didn't try to stop him. So I yelled out, " Why yall aint stop him? " Someone in the crowd said that was your job and they continued to play as my opponent yelled his point. Nine! Now even though he would go on to later win the game I can surely tell you that I was one of the ones left in the game with twelve points.

Participating in these functions with the boys is just what I needed to make me more rougher around the edges. At times I thought that I was tougher than some of the boys. Anytime I had the chance and the boys decided to include me I would play. Later learning that these activities was also helping me with my anger management and it was giving me different avenues to channel and change my negative feelings into positive results.

Family Traits

My older brother was always in the streets, out and about doing something. When I would go over to my mother's house, I would have to wake up bright and early to catch him before he left the house. Or I would be subject to being the "in house" babysitter whom doesn't get paid by the way because these are my siblings. She was always in the streets or locked away in her bedroom with her man. During the summer of 2000, my mother resided on the Eastside of Detroit in a three bedroom house on the block of Fordham and Hayes with my older brother, my three younger sisters and was pregnant now with a boy. I didn't know she was pregnant because it had been a minute since I had been over to her house.

We had fallen out over me not wanting to babysit. She was so petty that she went over to my adopted mother's house and told her some of the things that she had read in one of my diaries and of some things she "thought" I was doing. So I was punished by my adopted mother and part of my punishment was being grounded to the house. On the day I went over to visit, my mother informs me that she has a birthday gift for me and it is on the bed. I walk over to the bed and began to undress it only to uncover an infant baby. I looked back toward my mother and said there is no gift here and she informed me that the baby was my gift because he was born on my birthday. A couple days after I arrived, our other sister came to visit. (Our mother's fifth child but second girl.) Part of the first bunch of kids that were taken by the state but she was raised by her father's side of the family.

This was my first time being around my sister since we were in foster care meeting up at the agency. She was coming over to spend some of the summer break with the family. So we could get to know each other and create a bond. For a couple days she stayed very reserved and to herself because she really didn't know us know us. She just knew the things she was told so she didn't know how to react or open up to us.   After a few days she begin to come around the bend and open herself up. She broke down the wall that had her divided from us and begin to speak on her home life and what she went through on the daily basis. She informed me that she was being molested by her guardian's boyfriend. Her guardian was her aunt. She said that every time her aunt went to work she would leave the two of them home alone and that is when he would molest her. I was upset because I knew what molestation was and I knew how she felt by it happening to me before.

It was all too familiar. My sister was afraid to tell our mother because of the previous reaction that she received from her aunt, which was total disbelief until her aunt told her that if it did happen she probably wanted it to happen because she was hot in the ass. So I went and told her. I felt as if it was my duty to tell someone so our sister could be protected. I felt it was up to our mother to protect her since her aunt didn't and wasn't doing so. Once our mother found out she had a conversation with my sister about it and talked to the aunt about it but to my knowledge nothing was done. The aunt stood by and stayed with her man and our mother conducted herself as if nothing was said.

The aunt would let our sister spend the week with us then of acting out. One time I awoke to her having a loud conversation with another kid from the block but by me just waking up I really didn't pay too much attention to what they were talking about. Plus they were kids so it couldn't have been too much of a big deal. Another time I woke up to find that she wasn't in the house so I ventured outside and begin to call her name in hopes that she was somewhere close but nope. The elderly neighbor that watched over the whole block and could tell you who was doing what with who, pointed down the block and said she with them boys. I instantly knew where she was. It was a little weed spot down the street that contained a lot of young boys as well as grown men. I marched down there with no hesitation.

No knocking on the door, I just walked right on through the house. One of the boys sitting in the dining room on two crates at the table bagging up asked what I was trying to get. I said nothing and begin to shout my sister's name. The boy then replied, "Oh she in the room," and pointed. So I followed the direction of where he pointed his finger and it lead me to a hallway where there were two bedrooms and a bathroom. One room to my left. One down the hall to my right with the bathroom directly in front of me. The bedroom to my left door was open so you could tell no one was in there. I walked toward the bedroom to my right where the door was closed and pushed it open. In this room I would find my sister being tugged and pulled on. Touched by at least several different boys who were yelling at her to show them "what it do." One boy even yelled that they were about to pull a "train" on her. Meaning that more than one person was going to fuck her at once. I ran into the room, grabbing my sister by her arm and pulled her out the room, out the house eventually dragging her down the steps of the residence but

33

she struggled with me like she wanted to get loose.
Like she wanted to be there and she wanted
whatever was going to happen to happen to her.

When we were finally outside I let her go only to
stand there and go back and forth with her about
me trying to be a big sister now. I slapped her in
her face as hard as I could for talking to me like that.
Like I had a choice in the matter. We were kids! So
she should 't be mad at me for what happen to us
and how we ended up. Wasn't my fault. After the
slap she grabbed her face and continued to be
rugged at the mouth. I told her to go to the house
she then told me that I couldn't make her so I
grabbed her by what little ponytail she had and
dragged her toward the house. All the while she
kicked and screamed.
When she got loose she ran off. I wasn't chasing
her so I went on to the house to call and tell our
mother what my sister had just got caught doing or
trying to do.

Our mother was in the streets so when I called she seemed unbothered by the information I was giving her so I really didn't press the issue over the phone. I really knew she wasn't bothered by the time she came home because she took her precious time getting there to check on her kids and the situation. That incident prompted for my sister to be sent home. Not for being in a house full of dudes but because she had ran away from the house and no one knew where she was until she came back of her own free will. Now that she was gone I could relax a little bit. Our mother ended up having some friends and family over so my older brother and I ventured down the street to his girlfriend Carrie's house. She stayed on the same block as our mother just on the opposite side and further down the street.

Carrie was already sexually active at the age of fourteen. We knew that because she had already had a baby. When we got down to her house I was left with the baby to baby sit while my brother and Carrie went upstairs to mess around. My boyfriend at the time whom would later become my child's father came over to my mother's house looking for me. My mother knowing where I was sent him down the street to me.   I heard the knock at the door and answered it.   When I heard who it was I opened the door.   With the baby being sleep on the couch we entered the downstairs bedroom which belonged to Carrie's parents.   While we were in the process of exploring one another Carrie's step-father walked in on us.   Caught us in the process of taking our clothes off.   He started yelling at us to get the fuck out of his house.   I gathered up my things and we ran out.   I ran to my mother's house and waited for them to follow.

It took a minute for them to come because the step-father waited for the mother to get home. Eventually they would come stomping down the block as if they were a marching band.   It was every bit of one to one thirty in the morning and all of a sudden all you hear is a lot of ruckess.   Announcing themselves before they even hit the door.   Now me, I had sat up all night and not said not a word or two to anybody in the house because I was too busy praying to GOD hoping that Carrie's parents wouldn't come down here but I guess that prayer was still on hold because here they were. They put on a big show and my mother followed right behind and assured them that this would be taken care of. That's all she said as she walked them out the door of the enclosed porch. When she entered back into the house, I was still sitting in the same spot from the time I first ran in.

Still not speaking no words. I knew I was in the wrong so what more could I do besides apologize for my behavior. My mother came at me with nasty looks as well as nasty words. Going all the way in. Ham, turkey bacon and with a few slaps across my face it was done and she was back into her room with her kids father. The next morning when she got up, my mother woke me up and told me to get dressed. Called me a cab and sent me over to my cousin's house on Three Mile Drive and East Warren, where my older brother was. My boyfriend stayed right around the corner on

Devonshire and Southhampton.   So he was just a hop away.   I called him.   We met up and basically finished what we had started the night before therefore in that moment conceiving our beautiful blessing of a daughter.

The Release Of The Gift

When I decided to lose my virginity I was twelve years old and just graduated eighth grade. I called myself knowing it all as the old folks would a say. I had two boyfriends at one time. I had a weekly boyfriend that I saw almost every day of the week and I had a weekend boyfriend that I would see when I went over to my biological mother's house. My weekly boyfriend and I had just recently gotten together and made an agreement that if we were together for thirty days or more I would let him take my virginity. My weekend boyfriend and I had been together almost three years at this time but we had never discussed having sex. So when the thirty days were up the weekly boyfriend was ready for his reward. He started planning and plotting on how we were going to do this and get away from everybody without getting caught.

We had set the scene up as many as three times but every time it was planned I got nervous and didn't follow through with meeting up with him.

Eventually after the three failed attempts , my weekly boyfriend broke up with me for the girl across the street from me. I was hurt and disappointed. Here I was thinking that my weekly boyfriend really liked me but all it seemed like he wanted was sex when I had a rider from the start. My weekend boyfriend never asked or pressured me about sex not even dry humping or the touchy feely thing so after much thought I decided that my weekend boyfriend would be the best recipient to receive my virginity. Plus, we had been together way longer. Working on like three to four years or so. I decided that the next time I saw my weekend boyfriend that it would happen. Sex that is! I would be the one to initiate it. This would lead us to the scene at my older brother's girlfriend Carrie's house.

Not Seen Clearly

Now my older brother was a well groomed and well maintained young man. Something like the super model type. Handsome and well built. He hustled, went to school and had a job. He took care of home as well as himself. When it came to females that wasn't a problem. He had them. All ages, all types in every hood near you. They were everywhere. He even had two females on the same block that our mother lived on. A couple doors down from each other. I would befriend girls to have them come over to my mother's house so that he could see them. I had three reasons for doing this. One being I was down for my older brother. I was Robin and he was Batman. Two being he didn't want to be seen bringing girls home because he already had two different girls on the block that may be watching him. Three because if one of his girls did just so happen to pop up he could say that she was my friend.

Once the girls saw him they would fall ever so deep in love with him. All he had to do give them some extra attention and bam it was over. He had them. One morning I was asleep on the couch which was located to the right of our mother's bedroom when she received a phone call. I could hear her going back and forth with whomever it was on the other end of the line about my older brother. After she hung up from the phone call she started talking to her kid's father about what she was just told. I only over heard the conversation because they talked so freely believing that it was early in the morning and they assumed everyone in the house was still asleep.

It was said that a paraplegic female, paralyzed from the neck down. Awoke from her sleep to find my older brother on top her with his pants down. Penetrating her. By just hearing the story and calling myself knowing my older brother I didn't first initially believe the story. I let it go in one ear and out the other as they would say. When my older brother arrived home he was pulled in our mother's

room to be questioned about the situation. He
denied everything and kept saying that it didn't
happen like that. In the moment after he said that
the phone rang, It was the girl's parents yelling
through the phone at our mother. Yelling about
how they were headed to the hospital to have their
daughter checked out, about if the story was true
that they were calling the police to have my older
brother arrested and prosecuted then hung up.

That was the last I would hear of this situation until
later on in the year. My older brother would start
keeping to himself and staying gone more. I
couldn't be concerned about him because I had
more important things to worry about. Like myself
and why I was eating and sleeping a lot. In
November, the police showed up at our mother's
house to arrest my older brother. I kept asking our
mother what had happened and what was going on
but she just never responded. She just stood there
as the police handcuffed my older brother and lead
him away down to the station. Not even following.
I continued to question our mother as to why she

wasn't doing nothing to help my older brother and she replied, "That it was none of my concern, that this was grown folks business and to stay out her face." I grew an attitude and left her house to return to my home where my adopted mother was.

Changes

I had already begin to show symptoms of pregnancy but me being a kid really not knowing anything. I didn't know that I was. I didn't too much understand the total meaning of fucking and or having sex I thought sex was more of the noise then the action. Meaning I thought people were having sex when they would make the noises of the oo's and aaa's. So when asked was I having sex I immediately would respond no because in my mind I didn't make enough noises to have had sex. Plus it was only two maybe three humps before it was over.

When I made it home to my adopted mother it seemed as if she picked up on my changes very quickly and started asking questions. Everything she asked I responded no to. That following weekend she would let me return to my biological mother's house. There were a couple incidents at my biological mother's house that had me questioning my health as far as what food and how much food I consumed. The sleeping spells and mood swings. Once I start paying attention to my body I noticed the changes happening. Where I was once flat or smooth all over now began to bud like flowers coming through the soil so I had a talk with my biological mother about the possibility of me being with child and she said it plain and simple like, "Oh you don't have to worry because if you are pregnant I'm taking you to get an abortion." So there it was and it was done. I had my answer and was satisfied with it.

I went home to my adopted mother I really thought no more of it until one morning my adopted mother asked me to ride with her while she ran errands so I did. Not knowing that this would be the day of my undoing. The first stop was dropping the other kids off at school then to the grocery store. When we pulled up to the grocery store my adopted mother handed me a list of items that she wanted. I got out the car to go in the store. As soon as I entered the grocery store I immediately smelled the odor of raw meat and it had me nausea. I tried to hold my composure and hold my breath so I couldn't smell anything but that only lasted so long. When I couldn't do it any longer I began to feel sick and ran toward the door for fresh air as well as a garbage can to throw up in. When I was finished vomiting I looked up to see my adopted mother watching me. Giving me that eye like, oh you thought you were slick.

We pulled out the parking lot of the grocery store and pulled up at Park Medical Doctor's office on Jefferson and Gray. I tried not to act nervous but I couldn't help it. I was too far gone. I followed all directions given. I gave a sample of my urine and end up in the examination room on the table, undressed getting ready for a pelvic exam. The doctor knocked at the door before entering the room. Once she entered the room the doctor gave my adopted mother this look and they both exited the room to stand outside the door. The doctor informed my adopted mother that my urine did test positive for being pregnant. I instantly burst out in tears hearing those words. It was finally confirmed. No more guessing or thinking. It was official. I was pregnant. My adopted mother entered back into the room and asked, "Why was I crying?" I didn't respond. I just continued crying. She then responded, "It's too late to start acting like a child now! You were grown enough to lay in that bed and spread your legs to make the baby now you gone be grown enough to stand on those same legs to raise this baby," and left the room. I got up to put my clothes back on.

Once I was dressed I exited the exam room and entered into the hall where my adopted mother was engaged in a conversation with the doctor and nurses. When I joined in the circle they got quiet and dispersed. The nurse assigned to my chart start questioning me about the conception and things of that sort. The nurse asked what were the plans. I replied, "I'm having an abortion." The look on everyone's face was mad shock, disbelief and disappointment. Then I looked toward my adopted mother. If looks could kill I would have been dead all the way back at the grocery store. This look was more like casket. I just shut my mouth and let my adopted mother give all the responses.

On the way to the van my adopted mother kept repeating to herself that she knew. On the ride home there no words spoken. I could feel the disappointment in the air. It was so thick you could choke on it like smoke. It was made up in my adopted mother's mind that this baby was going to be born but since I already had a conversation about this with my biological mother I was still planning to go through with the abortion. With or without permission. When we arrived home I went straight to my room to use the phone to inform all responsible parties. I called my weekend boyfriend to inform him. When he heard those words come out my mouth he was so excited that he blurted out that he meant to do it. I asked, "Do what?" He replied, "Get you pregnant. I meant to do it." I asked, "How?" Because we used a condom. I watched him put it on. He replied, "I took it off." I just hung up the phone. I couldn't believe that my weekend boyfriend had purposely chosen to get me pregnant by himself. With no input from me.

I was furious. He kept calling back until I answered the phone. He explained to me that he wanted the baby and I explained to him that I wasn't ready. He kept insisting that if I chose to have his firstborn child that he would be there for us, that he would do what he had to do to make sure the baby would be taken care of and have everything that it needs. He also explained to me how he wouldn't leave me to take care of the baby by myself, that he was going to be a great father. I was listening to him but I was not hearing anything that he was saying. I responded to him that he needed to give me some money toward the abortion. I was not having this baby, it was too soon for me. I was getting ready to start high school and didn't know where my life was headed. I just felt like I wasn't ready to have a baby.

At the end of our conversation we both had agreed upon the abortion no matter how he felt. I was putting my selfish reasons and feelings before him and our unborn child. At that moment in time I didn't care. I thought I was making the right decision based on me, my life and how this would affect my life. After I got off the phone with my child's father I called my biological mother to tell her the news. She didn't sound like she was surprised, she just said, "You know what you have to do." I told her that it was already in affect now all she had to do was convince my adopted mother to go along with the abortion plan but somewhere in the back of my mind I kind of knew she wasn't going to fall for no bullshit.

It took us almost two to three weeks to get my adopted mother to change her mind and support the abortion even though I believe it would still be done against her will even if she did not give the okay. Abortion was just something my adopted mother didn't believe in. She believe in the true sacrifice of giving what you have to others. That is where we came along into her life, through that belief. I knew I was disappointing my adopted mother but I tell you I thought I was doing what I needed to do to keep me straight. The first time I went into the abortion clinic it was in walking distance from my biological mother's house. The clinic was located on East Seven Mile and McCrary on Detroit's Eastside. In the back of this big ran down tan colored building. I didn't know it was located this close. Not even two blocks away. When we entered the building, there were some females already in the waiting room. We approached the counter, picked up a clip board and proceeded to be seated.

My biological mother filled out as much information on the paperwork as she could because she didn't know all the details of my life. When she was finished with what she did know she handed me the clip board to fill out the rest of the paperwork. After I had finished the clip board I returned it to the lady at the counter. She took the paperwork and then told me to have a seat. I would be called shortly. Not really thinking too much about the abortion and or the procedures that would be done to my body I went for my seat.

After being seated the secretary called one female back while escorting another out. The female coming from the back had an unpleasant look on her face that seemed as if she was screaming in pain. She was in such pain she could barely stand straight up or barely walk. The nurse had to assist her with taking a seat.

As she was being seated I noticed that she had a blood trail coming down the inside of her pants leg. I looked toward my biological mother to ask what was wrong with her and what had happened. My biological mother started to explain the procedure to me and I began to cringe. There would be a small incision meaning cut. Some type of instrument like a vacuum being stuck up inside of your vagina to suck the baby out of my womb. I was through. What I heard as well as what I saw had me scared. I couldn't stand the sight of blood and that had me feeling sick so I decided that on that day I wasn't ready. I changed my mind on having the procedure done that day but I still wanted the abortion.

We left only to return not even a week later. It took me that long to build up the courage I thought I needed to get this done. Anyhow I was ready. We arrived back at the clinic located in the back of the building. The nurse called me to the back where I was introduced to the doctor named, Dr. Pornpitcher. After the introduction, he explained to me what was going to happen, how long it would take and how I may feel afterwards but said everything would go as planned and the way I would feel after the procedure would be natural. Before we started the process Dr. Pornpitcher announced he wanted to do an ultrasound to determine my number of weeks or months pregnant so that he could then determine how much to charge me.

 While the doctor prepared myself as well as himself for the ultrasound he discussed the form of payment with my biological mother because I hadn't any clue what the price was going to be. I just knew that my child's father had just given her four hundred dollars the day we came down last week plus she supposedly had put some money with that as well as one of my aunts had given her a couple of dollars. So I thought I had nothing to be worried about. Dr. Pornpitcher started the ultrasound by placing a cloth over my bottom half, he put that cold ass gel on my stomach then added the scope. While grazing across my belly Dr. Pornpitcher did the doctor's usual hmm's and aa's then turned the screen my way so I could see the image of the baby that was growing inside of me.

As Dr. Pornpitcher glided the scope across my stomach he explained to me what he saw, what he was showing me and what we were doing. Dr. Pornpitcher explained the image of the baby's feet and hands saying that they were all there. He turned up the volume so I could hear the sound of the baby's heartbeat. The doctor then showed me the image of the baby's ear and said, "The baby has fully formed hands, feet, everything even with a sounding heartbeat. It is no longer a fetus but now a human being. To abort this child would be like killing an actual living human being." I guess in hopes of persuading me to change my mind but my mind was already made up and had been made up from the first time I even considered thinking to myself that I could have been pregnant.

Dr. Pornpitcher than announced that I was twenty to twenty one weeks pregnant pushing more toward twenty one weeks. He determined that he was going to charge almost eight hundred dollars. I was like, "What?" Dr. Pornpitcher then explained his reasoning for his decision. Which was based on the idea of killing an actually living human being like he was really against it. If that was the case why was he even in this field of study or in this business. After Dr. Pornpitcher's quick explanation he said he would give my biological mother and I a moment so we could discuss what we were going to do. I asked the doctor not to leave the room, turned toward my biological mother and told her I was ready. My biological mother then responded to Dr. Pornpitcher and asked if he could drop the price because she only had one hundred ninety four dollars on her. My mouth dropped and hit the floor along with my face.

  What the fuck did she mean she only had? She only had what? My child's father gave her four hundred and she didn't even have that. What the fuck was she thinking or not thinking? My biological mother had really flipped the script asking Dr. Pornpitcher to drop his price like she was ant where near the amount he was asking for. What the fuck was she trying to do put my abortion on lay-a-way? I was done for. I started to get dressed. I fastened my clothes, got off the table and headed toward the door. Too pissed to speak any words I returned home to inform my adopted mother as to what had happened. She responded, "I could've told you so but you want to be so grown and keep following behind your mother. You will see and sure enough learn one of these days that she ain't no good for you but that is for you to figure out. I can't keep telling you and I'm not. That is the reason you are here with me. If she wanted you she would have you or got herself together to get you all back."

Now I was hurt and disappointed. I didn't know where to turn or who to talk to. My biological mother had really let me down a lot in the situations where I really was depending on her to come through and my adopted mother felt some type of way because she felt as if I was following behind and choosing my biological mother over her. So I retreated into myself. The only place I could find pure silence. Pure peace. Pure solitude.

What's Done In the Dark

Upon me entering into the house the occupants of the house were already engaged in a conversation about what they had just seen on the television. When I entered the room it became very quiet and the family just stared at me until I asked what was the problem then my little cousin yelled out, "Your mom and brother was on the news. They in jail because your brother was fucking your sister." I stood there as if a statue. Frozen in time. I gasped for air as if I couldn't breathe and said, "What?" I couldn't believe what I was hearing. It couldn't be true. I was so concerned. Concerned for my family and loved ones. Concerned for myself. What the fuck was going on? What if my friends watched the news? The teachers? The haters? OMG! I didn't know what to do, what to think or where to start.

I ran upstairs to my room and buried my face in my pillow full of tears. Eventually my adopted mother came up the stairs to check in on me. Asking me questions but at the same time assuring me that whatever happened was not my fault nor was it a reflection of me. I told her that it didn't happen to me or our sister. I was explaining all the reasons why I thought he couldn't have done this. One reason was because he had so many other girls that he was fucking. I was all in his defense. Going on and on. She just looked at me. I started with, "How could this be happening?" and begin to sob all over again. My adopted mother left me to be by myself since she couldn't find the words to console me. I stayed in my room all night, I didn't want to see or talk to anyone. Nor did I want to eat, get anything to drink or even go to the bathroom.

The next day in school I kept to myself as well. I had not a clue if people had seen the story about my biological mother and older brother. The whole day no one said anything of the sort. By the time I made it home I was ready to talk so I went directly to my adopted mother to ask her the questions because I knew she didn't hold no punches. I asked her, "Why did they take my mother?" and my adopted mother responded, "Because she knew." I was taken aback by the comment because in the back of my mind I still don't want any of this to even be true. Back then we had the internet but very few knew how to work it if they messed with it at all. I didn't know anything about googling the story so I sat up all day and all night until they played the snippet of the story again. When I saw the pictures of their mug shots my mouth dropped.

The same story my adopted mother told me was the same story the anchor was reporting. Channel Four even went as far as to send David Scillian to the hood to interview the children's father at the house. It was almost like a drive by with cameras. The clip showed the kids playing outside and when the father spotted the news truck coming up the street, he grabbed all the kids and rushed them in the house. Locking the door. The newscaster showed every angle of that brown house with blue trim around the windows as he yelled questions at the windows and suggested for him to come out to answer these questions. I was devastated and embarrassed because it had to be some kind of truths to the story for the police to arrest both of them.

Reguardless, I still chose to attend their court dates with all the news media and presence in Thirty Six District Court. Through the proceedings is where I gathered the majority of my information since no one in the family was talking about it and or seemed to know. I found out the reason all this came about was because our sister had become sick and was showing symptoms of being pregnant so one of her school administrators gave her a pregnancy test which would return with the results being positive. Our sister was then taken to the hospital where she was administered a rape kit and Child Protective Services were contacted due to her only being the age of eleven. When questioned about what had happened to her and who had done this to her she answered it was our older brother. She said that she wasn't a willing participant and that this was forced on her. She said that this/it had been going on since she first came by and it would almost happen daily in the household of our biological mother.

Our sister said that our older brother would threaten her not to tell by tell her that he would do harm to her and or to the people that she love. Sometimes even brandishing a knife to show he was serious. Our older brother said that it only happened twice. Hold up, hold up, hold up! It only happened twice? It wasn't supposed to be happening at all. Our older brother story was that he came home after being in the streets all day drinking and was tipsy so when he made it to his room he passed out in his bed. He woke up to the feeling of someone on top of him straddling him. When he came to he realized that it was our sister and pushed her off of him, the report has him quoted as saying and then she stormed out.

 The next incident would take place he says because she kept threatening him with telling our biological mother that he was raping her. After that incident he would try his best to stay away from the house while she was over, the report continues. So the case was labeled incest, which is sex with a close relative and the State Of Michigan granted and paid for our sister to have an abortion. So she did. Our brother was charged with two counts of Criminal Sexual Conduct in the third degree meaning with a person/child under the age of thirteen. This crime was two counts of nine to fifteen years imprisonment he was facing at the age of fifteen.

High School

Entering the ninth grade at Osborn High School on East Seven Mile Road and Hoover Street on Detroit's Eastside, I was pregnant. I had become with child over the summer of 2000 by my weekend boyfriend my very first time having sex. With all that was going on I didn't trust anyone so I kept to myself. I've always been a smart cookie especially when I decided to use my brain, other than that a lot of stuff was simple. My favorite subjects were anything that challenged me to be creative and use my mind like Math, English-Language Arts and anything Science.

I would eventually befriend this guy named Otis Woods who would later become my crutch. Otis and I had the majority of our ninth grade classes together. Once we became friends we would sit beside each other and help each other out in class. While we were in the lunchroom, Otis would get in line to get his lunch and when the line moved up I would jump in front of him. After receiving our lunch we would find a place to sit and eat on the left side of the lunchroom all the way in the back along the wall. On this particular day Otis was watching me too intensely and finally asked about my eating habits saying, "You eat the school lunch, bring a lunch from home and have snacks that you eat but it seems like you aint gaining no weight.   What you pregnant or something?"   I was in the process of taking a bite out of my slice of pizza when he asked the question and he really didn't give me a chance to respond before he said, "You are," with a little of glee in his voice as if this was his baby or something.

Otis then grabbed his notebook, snatched out a sheet of paper and begin to write down baby names for boys as well as for girls.   When he finished he handed the piece of paper over to me and told me to keep it so I could read it later.   This is how I would later come up with my baby's name.   I would take the first two names on the list to create my child's name when I found out I was having a girl. My child's father was elated that I would be keeping the baby.   I would be the one to bring his first born seed into this world.   I would eventually turn the tide of my own feelings about my pregnancy as well. I begin to look at my pregnancy as a blessing from GOD because after all that was done to try and get rid of the baby GOD was doing everything in HIS power to make sure that this baby would be born. To make it here to walk and breath amongst us.

I had a baby shower that nobody came to.   Either because they didn't know I was pregnant or the people who did know was too disappointed to even deal with me but to the few that did show and bring gifts, I, we, still thank you.   My daughter, her father and I thank you and truly appreciated the support. Also a special thank you to you as well Mr. Otis Woods wherever you may be on this earth.   Thank you.   I attended high school throughout my entire pregnancy until I could no longer fit into my regular clothes.   I really didn't have a belly.   The baby bump I did have would always be covered by a sweater.   When it got closer to my due date my adopted mother took me out of school.   I would not

even miss a whole two weeks after my daughter
was born before I returned to school.

The Birth Of A New Chapter

Once I decided to accept my baby and the fact that I was going to be a teenage mother everything from that moment on would be smooth sailing. My biological family was in turmoil buy my home life with my adopted mother was great. It seemed as if the pregnancy had brought us even closer than we initially were in the beginning. The night I went into labor, of course I didn't know I was in labor I just felt uncomfortable and tight pinching in my pelvic area from time to time. It was a Thursday night and the whole adopted family was over competing in a tournament of Spades. I was on the winning team, sitting down at the table when the discomfort started. I would eventually exit the game the winner I am to go lay down in bed. Only to find that I couldn't get comfortable no matter what I tried.

I couldn't even sleep. After using the bathroom I cleaned myself to discover that I had some type of mucus looking discharge coming from me. I put a sanitary napkin on not knowing if it would continue or get heavy. I didn't know nor did I inform anyone of what was happening. When my adopted mother finally came upstairs to go to bed around two something in the morning I told her that I wasn't feeling good and how I felt I couldn't describe. My adopted mother told me to return to my room and she would check upon me in the morning to see how I felt so I did. The pinching pain in my pelvic area now had turned into cramps and had me feeling as if my bottom half was going to fall off. When morning came I still hadn't been to sleep and by now I couldn't keep any food down.

The pain was increasing and now there was a pressure pushing on my pelvic area almost feeling like I was about to have a bowel movement. I explained this to my adopted mother and she just replied, "Well if it feel like you have to shit don't push because you might tense up and end up with hemorrhoids or the baby in the toilet but it could just be them Braxton Hitchcocks." I repeated what she said, "Braxton Hitchcock? Who is that?" My adopted mother responded, "That's them false contractions. If you are in labor you need to walk that baby down because I'm not about to be running back and forth to the hospital over Braxton's." She told me to ride with her and we were out in the world.

 We dropped the kids off at school. Handle some of her business. We went bed shopping to end up with bund beds. We went to the grocery store. We went to a business office where she had to see a lawyer. We were some of everywhere. I t was a busy business Friday. All the while we were riding around, my adopted mother listened to her Peggy Scott Adams cassette with the volume turned all the way up so she couldn't or didn't have to hear my cries of pain. Laid all the way in the back of the van on the reclined bed. After all the business was handled my adopted mother told me to call my biological mother and inform her that I was headed to the hospital. I did so and called my child's father as well only to find out that he was in jail.

When we arrived at Hutzel Women's Hospital located in the John R and Canfield area, my adopted mother dropped me off at the entrance and told me to wait on her until she found a parking spot. I don't know how many minutes it took per say but I knew it felt like forever because I had at least three contractions going on four when she made it back to me. My adopted mother left me at the entrance of the hospital so when I started having another contraction two nurses rushed to my aid asking questions but all I could say in between the contractions were I have to wait on my adopted mother. When she finally did arrive back at the entrance with me, the nurses escorted us into the lobby and up to the desk. Coaching me on my breathing as well as my pain tolerance level.

Once all information needed was given I was sent straight to the delivery room to get undressed. My adopted mother followed of course. Once behind that curtain I became frozen like a statue. I did not want to get undressed in front of her because I didn't want her to discover that I had on a sanitary napkin. My adopted mother spoke life into me with the tine of her voice. Asking, "What was taking me so long?" I instantly came to life. I begin by explaining the mishap of the sanitary napkin as I started to get undressed. When my adopted mother saw the pad she asked how long I had it on and I explained to her that I had it on all day. My adopted mother explained to me in detail that the mucus was a sure sign that I was in labor and that it was a part of my water breaking but my water had not broken yet. Once undressed I put on the hospital gown that was issued and got upon the table to be examined.

By that time my biological mother was coming through the door with one of my little sisters. Rushing to my side to aid in the delivery of my baby. The nurses were back and forth in and out the room checking on my progress. One nurse informed me that my OB doctor was contacted and on his way down to deliver the baby. Another nurse joked and said the doctor said don't have the baby until he gets here but I wasn't hearing any of that. A film crew even came in and asked could they record my delivery for some program to be aired in television. I said no! I hadn't told anybody that I was pregnant and I didn't want them to find out through television. I didn't want my situation broadcast around the world. It was a for sure no.

After the film crew left, a nurse entered the room to check my cervix. I did not feel anything. Not even the pressure coming from the inside of my body. I did not feel her hand or anything but I knew she was inside of me. When the nurse had finished she informed us that I was eight and a half centimeters dilated but my water wasn't broke. Eight centimeters was a great number. I was ready and able to give birth vaginally verses the c-section. The nurse left the room only to return to the room with a long thin stick that looked like and was thin like a tooth pick but the stick had a hook on the end of it. The nurse informed us what she was getting ready to do. How she was going to insert this instrument up inside me to grab ahold to the sack and puncture it to release the fluids so I could officially be in labor.

No sooner than the nurse did that my water was broken the contractions and the pain increased and became closer together. Before the nurse left the room she coached me on what to do when my contractions became two to three minutes apart. No sooner then she left a contraction started. I did exactly as she had told me to do. By this time my adopted mother had left the hospital with my younger sister to finish handling her business. It was just my biological mother and I. My biological mother was trying to comfort me and touch me but I wasn't having it. I was bothered in the worst way. No one had explained this to me. None of it. From the beginning to the end. From boyfriend to girlfriend to the birds and the bees.

I had skipped over everything and now was going straight to pushing the baby's carriage. Everything was really happening. I was about to be a teen mother. A satistic of many not destined to make it anywhere. The walls were closing in on me. I could hardly take a breath. Shit was real! After the nurse left the contractions started again, my biological mother was on the sideline yelling, telling me what to do. I was sitting up with the bed propped back a little so when the contractions started I grabbed the back of both my thighs, pulled them toward my body as if trying to put your legs behind your head, put my chin to my chest and begin to push hard. Grunts, farts and all.

 My biological mother yelled, "Look!" In the same position that I was in, I opened my eyes to look down only to see a little head coming out my vagina. I screamed, "What the fuck?" and stopped pushing. In my mind I had just died and came back to life because me being a child no one explained any of this to me. I had taken it upon myself to conclude a lot of things. Like in this instance I was dead. I had died because I thought that the baby would come out the ass. I don't know why but that is what I thought. Don't blame me I was only a kid. Anyhow, another reason I thought this was reassured by the nurses when I told them that I needed to or felt like I had to boo-boo, have a bowel movement, they informed me that it was the pressure of the baby pressing down on my pelvic. Coming back to life in the delivery room I hear screaming. My biological mother is telling me to keep pushing as she runs to the door to yell for the nurses. No sooner than she did that I heard the voice of my OBGYN. His voice was calming. He was telling me to relax and get ready for the biggest push. I told him I couldn't. I was physically exhausted.

We went back and forth few times until he explained to me that if I didn't push her out that she was going to die. The baby had the umbilical cord wrapped around her neck twice. I was basically suffocating her. With those words, I summed up all that I had in me and released my blessing upon this world. When I begin to push my OBGYN grabbed my blessing by her neck and snatched her out of me. Quickly unraveling the umbilical cord to give my blessing air so she could have life. I just lay there lifeless. When she took breath so did I.

My blessing was a new life and had given me new life. With no words I just laid there. I looked at her as she looked back at me while the doctor gave me three invisible stitches.   Yup she ripped me but what such a beautiful tear.

Back To School

Besides Otis Woods guessing that I was pregnant, the only person that I had told besides my biological mother and my child's father was my girl best friend whom lived down the street from us at the corner of Saratoga and Reno. My boy best friend which lived across the street from me didn't even know or notice. I arrived home two days after having my daughter I phoned my boy best friend to tell him the news. Over the phone we went back and forth about this being a joke of some sort. He said that he didn't believe me and he wouldn't believe me until he saw it with his own eyes. So I invited him over. When he walked through the door I was sitting on the couch holding my daughter. His mouth just hit the floor. Now that everyone important to me knew my secret I felt more comfortable when I returned to school. I had only been out not even two weeks altogether. Before and after the birth of my daughter and up until those days I had not missed not one day.

When I returned the teachers as well as a few students were curious as to where I had been for those two weeks. I came prepared for that with a written absence excuse but the majority of all my teachers told me that it was fraudulent. They called home but the number the school had on file was from so long ago that the telephone number was disconnected so they got no answer. I would have to be escorted into the school by my adopted mother and my daughter along with all paperwork and documentation stating that this was my baby. Everyone in the office was stunned! But as soon as they laid eyes upon my baby everyone was in love. Every day someone if not everyone asked about my daughter and her well-being. It seemed to become the normal. Life that is, had quieted down. There was nothing left to be said. Everything had been spoken. Now there was nothing but peace, stillness and quietness.

By the tenth grade it seemed as if I had everything under control. Taking care of my daughter, school and household duties. I was practically doing this with my arms tied behind my back and my eyes closed. There was nothing too difficult for me to learn or understand. Once it was explained I basically got the hang of it. With Fall approaching we prepared to go back to school. As usual with me being a child, I couldn't wait to go school shopping. Again informed that all the funds usually used toward or for me would now be used for the baby. I had heard that line before during Christmas time of 2000.

I had plotted out my Christmas list of the things I wanted. When I finished I took the list to my adopted mother. She took the piece of paper. Looked at it, read it, looked back at me and laughed very Dr. Evil'ly. I just stood there. Confused? I couldn't figure out what I had put on the list was so funny. My adopted mother then turned to me as if she heard the thought running through my head to answer the question I had asked myself. My adopted mother said to me, "You don't get nothing for Christmas anymore. Everything will be used for the upkeep of the baby." I was fine with that as long as my baby was taken care of. Wanting, needing or lacking of anything.

I was happy until school started back. I had not anything to wear but the maternity clothes I had worn last year to conseal my pregnancy. My baby was born now and all of whatever weight I had gained was gone. The clothes I had were extra big and bulky on me now. I had to do something. I had to find a way to get some money. To get some clothes. I needed new clothes and I definitely needed my own money so I turned to the only thing I knew best. The things my older brother taught me and that was hustling.

The first thing I did was advertise that I was doing hair. I landed a few neighborhood girls who came to me on the weekly basis to receive twisties, braids or a simple ponytail. I would take the money I made from doing hair and gamble with it. Starting with my family and later expanding to the people of the neighborhood. Gaining the funds from gambling I was able to provide for myself as well as

82

my daughter. So I continued. I was too young to legally obtain a job so hustling it was.

It would take me almost a year or so to start back liking boys and having sex. I was too focused on getting money to make sure that we had. My daughter and I that is. At that age nobodies mind was on getting money. Kids were so use to their parents, grandparents or family providing everything. Their wants and their needs but I had none of that. I had to provide for two. Kids minds were on being fresh and keeping up with the latest fashion or whatever was popular at that moment. I was focused on keeping my daughter fresh and with all she needed and wanted. My mind was always on something else because I had more responsibilities than the other kids my age. Plus, I was still afraid to let a boy touch me because I thought he would try to get me pregnant as well.

Hustling came easy as well. Like knowing the back of your hand. With hustling I had money for my clothes, shoes, etc. I had money to buy my daughter clothes, shoes, diapers and formula. I had money to help out around the house. I had money was the best and most important part. I had the money to buy whatever it was I thought I wanted or needed. I felt the same about my daughter. Anything I wanted her to have she had. My adopted mother was curious as to where the funds were coming from. I would just tell her that I had braided someone's hair or something like that and she would leave it alone.

The summer I turned sixteen I met an older gentleman who was very into me. When he learned my age he backed up and told me he was willing to wait on me until I turned legal. But told me that whatever I needed or wanted that I couldn't afford even if it was just something I wanted to call him and he would make it happen. I already knew what he wanted from me as far as sex but he was willing to wait for me to turn eighteen to get it from me so I was good with that situation.

When I started hustling I begin to attract people of like minds. At the age of sixteen I was kicking it with DT. DT was eighteen years old. He was a good six feet. Dark skin in complexion with brown eyes. He was a solid one hundred seventy five pounds and wore a fade haircut. He was very stocky and built from the juvenile boot camp he was previously released from. DT would be my second boyfriend but the third guy I had sex with. We had a great relationship. I was drawn to him by his ambition to make it happen despite what he had been through in his childhood. DT was in the "Game of the Streets" and that was his way of providing for himself as well as his family. I admired his drive more than anything. We did things that regular couples did.

We went to movies, out to eat, down by the water and even pamper dates. I met his parents and family. I was happy in this relationship not knowing the unknowing would be our undoing. I didn't find out my boyfriend was a bank robber until the V.C.T.F., F.B.I., D.P.D., A.T.F., and all other alphabet boys raided my biological mother's house. They had already raided my adopted mother's house looking for my boyfriend and I. My adopted mother sent the police right to where I was. She didn't play that. The FEDS gave me so much unknown information that I was unaware of that I was now scared. Scared because I knew that the situation was serious and that the FEDS did not play when it came down to armed fugitives. Now DT was on the run.

Things That Come With A Price

My biological mother didn't question me not one
time about anything.   As long as she got what she
wanted out the situation or from a person she was
good.   As long as she could milk the cow, live on the
farm for free and drink the milk she was cool.   I first
started buying little things around the house like
toilet paper, toothpaste, soap and dish washing
liquid.   Then moved up from cigarette, gas money
to groceries and bills.   Going as far to buying some
people their own personals no matter what it was.
Cigarettes, weed, beer, liquor or whatever their
personal vice was.

I had even made it over to the major leagues where
everyone would borrow money from me with a date
of expectancy to pay it back.   But we all know how
black folks are.   I was even promised the famous
Judge Mathis line, that Ill get paid when they
receive their income tax.   Knowing damn well they
were never going to give me back my money.
Those are the people I learned from.   I learned how

to deal with them.   During this time I still had a child's mind.   I wasn't thinking in the full term or the future of things.   I was thinking of right now, then and there in the moment.   I went shopping at the mall all the time.   Going out to the movies. Skating, bowling, to the arcade and things of that such when I could have been saving and stacking. Stacking and saving.

In addition to hustling, going to school at the age of sixteen, I also had a side job as a shampoo girl working for Mr. Little himself.   The Icon.   The Legend.   The owner of Better Fashion's Hair Salon which was located on East Seven Mile and Teppert. I had been introduced to a nail tech working at Mr. Little's salon through a mutual good friend to start working with her as a hand model.   After seeing me a couple times Mr. Little asked if I'd be interested in being a shampoo girl and I said yes.   It gave me something extra to do and it was an easy form of money.   With Osborn being right down the street I would sometimes skip school to go up to Better Fashions or just wait until after school to go there before I went home. While spending so much time in the salon Mr. Little soon offered me the opportunity to become a model.

Working with Mr. Little as a model I was traveling to perform at hair competitions across the United States. During my senior year in high school a lot of things would begin to go haywire. My attitude had started to decline. No matter how much money I had or was making it wasn't making me happy. I was so busy taking care of others and what they wanted me to do. I felt as if I looked out for them that they would lookout for me. That wasn't true. As long as I had money I would have people around me who needed it so they would make it seem as if they had my back or so I thought but that wasn't even the case. It seemed like the more money I had the more people wanted from or required of me. I was doing and giving all that I had. All that I could but it still wasn't enough. I was being broken. Taken advantage of. Any or every time I needed something or someone I had to pay for it.

So my attitude had become fucked up by the way I was being treated and by the way I was thinking. I had met my Chaldean friend a few weeks before the summer. He followed me from the gas station on East Seven Mile and Hoover down to the liquor store on Runyon and Seven Mile. The Chaldean came into the store introduced himself to me and asked me where I was headed to. I told him the salon. The Chaldean placed something in my hand while shaking it. Told me to call him, turned around and left out the store. Once the Chaldean was gone I immediately opened my hand to find a fifty dollar bill balled up. When I unraveled it he had his number written on it. I went down to the lottery station, wrote the number down and broke the fifty dollar bill. I met my Chaldean on a Wednesday, by Friday he was taking me on a expense paid shopping spree in Chicago arriving back on Sunday.

A few days shy of my eighteenth birthday my adopted mother put me out her house after we had a verbal confrontation where I was being disrespectful. I called my biological mother. She came to pick up me and my things. We returned to where she was residing ,which was on Annchester and West Six Mile. My biological mother lived with her boyfriend or male friend who looked out for her from time to time. I really appreciated them for letting us come stay with them. Just after a few days it became apparent that the situation wasn't good and it wasn't going to last.

 Since I had arrived on the scene my biological mother's actions had changed, said her boyfriend. She was hanging in the streets more and lying. My biological mother and her boyfriend began to argue almost constantly to where she would want to leave the house. Me not knowing him, I would leave with her to end up having a full day and returning home in the late hours of the night. When we left we would have to pack everyone up. My biological mother had four other kids plus me and mine. I would pay for the food to feed us and the gas being put in the car to ride around all day from people to place to thing.

After the arguments started between my mother and her boyfriend, I kept hearing my name being thrown in it like I was the influence. I called my Chaldean, told him the story of what was happening and what I was going through. He assured me not to worry, that he was willing to help me with whatever I needed. The next morning my Chaldean came to pick us up. Took me to drop my daughter off to her father then took me to get a room. Once everything was handled we checked in the room , we sat down to have a very real and personal conversation. My Chaldean would give me my stepping stones to moving up in the game. My Chaldean would school me. Teaching me the rules of the game(s) he was in. He would set up trips for me to take to make plays. Either taking it to a destination or bringing it from a destination back to him. No matter whatever "it" was.

During these trips my Chaldean would send me with money and pay me money upon my return. It was another hustle added. The wage was more. Bigger than anything I had done before. I had moved on up to the big leagues and wasn't even paying any attention. My Chaldean had taught me the dice game called, "Four, Five, Six or Big Man's Money." One night while over to his people house they had started up a game where I watched him win almost a hundred thousand cash. I only know because I was there as well as I was the one who helped him count the money on the floor at the room and rubber band it. The most important thing my Chaldean taught me was that change can happen if and when you want it to. It's all up to you to make the first step. The first move of making it happen.

My Chaldean told me once, he said, "It's okay being comfortable in your surroundings when you don't know no better. When you know better you are not supposed to be comfortable with your surroundings." He said, "Pay attention, whether you understand it now or figure it out later. It's better to have the knowledge of the known then the unknown. You want to be a no body? Keep hanging around, dealing with the people you deal with. You are guaranteed to be a nobody but hang around people that are doing something. Anything. Getting money and you are bound to pick up something and learn something at the end of the day. It all depends on you!" All the motivation I needed to start to change my life, the things I was doing and the people I was dealing with.

Determined To Change

The summer of 2004 I bounced around from room to room with no stability. The only thing that gave me peace and solitude was the fact that I knew my daughter didn't have to go through this with me because her father had taken her for the summer. When I wasn't out of town I was with my Chaldean or at the room. When I wasn't doing either of those two things I was out in the streets hanging with my mother. Everyday and everywhere we went it was a party. That summer the party and I had become one. I was the party. I came with my own everything. What I didn't have or wanted I could buy or pay for so it wasn't a problem for me and sure as hell wasn't a problem for others when they didn't have to buy, pay or contribute to the party to gain access.

I was supposed to have a hotel party for my eighteenth birthday with friends, family and maybe even some foes. I canceled that event to have a

family party. My biological mother, her mother –

my granny, and my younger brother right after me –

also one of the children adopted by our adopted

mother belonging to my biological mother. At the

end of the night my mother took my brother home.

She had to leave to make it back to her nigga so that

just left grandma and I. I was disappointed. Hurt

by her at that very moment. Even then she chose

her nigga over spending time with her child on her

birthday. My granny could see the pain in my face

and came to embrace me. At the moment I

received that love I couldn't help but breakdown.

Crying cats and dogs.

I couldn't control them and they wouldn't let me

go. I laid all that I was feeling and had felt my

whole life right on the hotel room table. My granny

tried explaining some things to me. Only the things

she could. Now that my biological mother was

grown and even as a young teenager my biological

mother and my granny's relationship was strained.

Very tense. I believe that my biological mother

was like that with almost everybody or at least the ones she knew wasn't and didn't care about kissing her ass. Sometimes my biological mother would suck up to you just to use you to get whatever it is she wanted. To me it just seemed that she was always negative and into some kind of drama. Even as a young kid, from listening to the stories my granny would tell. My mother was a very disobedient as a child.

My granny worked so that left my mother home with her two older brothers and grandpa. Leaving my mother to witness, experience and even participate in despicable things that she wouldn't even have the courage to talk about let alone admit what had happened to her or that she knew about. My mother was so proud in herself that whatever happened to her as a child, kid, teenager or even adult she wouldn't mumble a word about it. It was some kind of secret that she felt that only they knew and wasn't supposed to tell nobody. When I say "they" I'm talking of all the ones who partook of any of these things that did happen to her. The more my granny talked the some what kind of understanding I was beginning to form. Some things were becoming clear to me. I was starting to be able to see why my mother was the way that she was.

I started to understand why my mother thought the way that she did as if everyone was against her or as if this was war. My granny was explaining and breaking everything down to me so I could form some type of understanding. To see things as they are instead of seeing things for what I wanted them to be. My granny also told me to start living for myself and to start only worrying about myself. Granny said it would be a good thing for me to just focus on self because I wasn't going to be able to get nowhere with my mother. Granny said it would be a waste of time trying because that's just the way she was. My mother was not willing to change herself, her actions or her mentality. Not for herself and not even for her kids. She hadn't done it all this time even when faced with the possibility of losing her kids she didn't reverse. Something I learned over time is that you cannot make another person do what they don't want to do. I knew that much. I wasn't slow to the program. I knew that my mother wasn't going to change unless she wanted to do it. Granny did do the consoling that night. Held me tightly in her bosoms and wiped away my tears. I will forever love her for that.

I had somewhat given my mother a pass somewhere in the back of my mind. I felt for her. I felt bad for her. I kind of knew what she went through only because the similar thing had happened to me as a child. I felt her pain. I just thought that since no one spoke of the incident that happened to me that no one knew of it and I had been the only person it had happened to. I was a child but I knew that the family very seldomly talked to each other so I didn't know if they had discussed the incident. I thought that the family wanted me to keep it to myself as if it was some type of secret. I thought that the family was using this silence so that later they could have the defense that the incident either didn't happen or that they had no knowledge that the incident had happened.

 Almost like what happened or was happening in the case with my older brother. How some people sugarcoated the incident by just saying he was away or in the military when in all actuality he was in prison for the rape of his sister. When I awoke in the morning I had a whole new outlook on the situation and relationship with my mother. I even had a new outlook on life period. It was time for me to change a couple things about and inside of myself. I wanted to become the person, the parent I know I was destined, determined and wanted to be. I had to start focusing more on my daughter and myself.

By the middle of August my biological mother and my younger siblings were living with me in the rooms at the hotel because my biological mother chose not to go back home to where she lived on Annchester and West Six Mile. With me providing and paying for the rooms I had to find the cheapest so we ended up staying between the Heritage Inn on East Eight Mile and Mohican. Across from the Reuben House and the Eastland Motel on Gratiot and East Eight Mile across from Dollar Tree. After feeding everyone and making sure they were settled my biological mother would let me take her car to go out and hustle. When I arrived back at the room I noticed the door was cracked to where I didn't have to knock to get in so I took it upon myself to enter the room. When I walked in all the kids were up getting ready for school while our mother lay in one of the beds with her bare assed nigga.

I didn't speak a word until I returned from dropping my siblings off to school. I didn't and wasn't putting no more gas into her car. I was leaving it on a quarter of a tank. I knew that would be a problem with her. Upon my return to the room I let my biological mother know I was down stairs waiting on her or them. They took their precious time coming down. They were probably fucking again now that the kids were gone. When I saw them exit the room I got out the driver seat to get into the back seat so her nigga could get in the front. Things seemed cool up until after she dropped her nigga off. Now all of a sudden she realizes she don't have no cigarettes , barely any gas and no money. Now she looks to me. I was prepared for the situation. I knew it would happen something similar to this. When she asked me to buy her a pack of cigarettes I answered quickly responding with sarcasm saying, "Why your nigga didn't buy you a pack?" My biological mother's face went from brown to red. I could actually see her top blow.

It had come straight off to reveal what little brain she did have. That is where the verbal confrontation started between us while she was driving. The argument had gotten so heated, that at one point she actually stomped on the break so hard to stop the car that the car jerked violently back and forth. Whatever my biological mother had to say to me at that time had to be intense. We were right around the corner from my daughter's father house so I just hopped out the car to leave her shouting at herself. Now her foot was on the break, the car wasn't in park, when I hopped out the car the car took off. I took it as she was trying to take off while I was getting out the car and even after I was out the car the argument continued.

 I was walking and my mother was riding alongside me with her passenger window down just shouting and being belligerent. I continued walking to where I was headed all the while. Speaking salutations to the residents who were outside to witness this rant. My biological mother followed me all the way to my child's father's house then continued bout her way. I gathered some clothes from my child's father's house. When my adopted mother put me out I had stored my daughter things as well as my things over to his house while I experienced my trials and tribulations.   It would be a couple weeks before I spoke to or saw my biological mother again. I knew she wouldn't be back around until she wanted to party or needed something. That is just how it was. That is just how she was or is.

On one occasion my biological mother and I were over to my aunt's (my mother's baby sister) house chilling and partying right before school started back. Doing what I had considered to become the usual on the daily basis. In between shots of eighteen hundred silver liquor, my mother and I ended up getting into an argument. She felt that we were teaming up on her. I was supposed to be on her side, on her team because I had come with her. During the confrontation of my mother cussing me out in front of everyone. She was jumping all up in my face. My aunt would try to put a wedge between us to try to calm the situation down but it didn't seem to be working.

As soon as my aunt got in between us things seem as if they escalated. Now my mother was saying that we were trying to double team her. The altercation now turned from my mother and I to my mother and her sister. The situation seemed to be getting out of control. My aunt had no other choice but to put her sister out her house. Demanding that my mother left her house immediately because of the commotion. All the while telling me I could stay. So I did. I could barely sleep that night. I had so much on my mind. I had to hurry up to get stable so I could get my daughter back where she belonged and that was with me, her mother. I resided with my auntie only for a few months before I moved in with my older boyfriend.

"KR" was at least eleven to twelve years older than me. While I was living with him I was introduced to government assistance I signed up. I didn't last that long in the Workfirst program because of the hours. I was doing almost thirty to fourty hour weeks for the little crumbs of two hundred three dollars a month. When I was doing the math I was confused. I know it didn't and wouldn't add up. I went to have a conversation with my adopted mother about the future of my life. My adopted mother didn't hold back no punches. She told it to you like it was and how she saw it not spearing anyone's feelings. The truth is the truth. Nothing to be ashamed of or nothing to apologize for. That was the part I loved most about her. She gave you the truth whether you liked it or not.

My adopted mother explained to me what she thought my downfall was and how to overcome it. She explained to me that the most important thing I could do for myself. As well as my daughter was get my life together. Keep it that way so I wouldn't have to depend on anybody. By the end of our discussion I was already etching out my blueprint of how to change my life in my mind. The next step would be to take the blueprint from my brain and make it into a reality. Over the next couple of months I would go through the trials of being in a cheating relationship but I wouldn't let that stop me from what I wanted for my daughter and I. During the process of obtaining all the knowledge I believed I needed to overcome all obstacles. Especially people. I would experience many difficult truths and realities. No more fairy tale stories with make believe characters and story plots. This was real. Real life. I believe I was told as a child growing up that a lot of people see the world through rose colored glasses. Never being able to see the world with clarity and understanding. I wanted that vision. I wanted that eye sight. I wanted to be able to see right through the world and especially its people. X-ray vision.

A Repeated Learning Process

After moving in with my aunt I would only be there not even three months before I left there to move in with my boyfriend who was thirty one years old at that time. "KR" was maybe five eight in height with a medium build and posture. Dark skin in complexion with brown eyes. I would end up in a relationship where I would be cheated on. Made to think that I was crazy for thinking and knowing. I was young and he thought I didn't know any better. Up until I found pictures of the two (my boyfriend and another female) out at the club in the bathroom together. Even at that moment my boyfriend still couldn't bring himself to admit to me that I wasn't crazy so I went crazy to show him the difference now that I knew the truth. I got to throwing and breaking things. I trashed the place. I even got to beating on him until he locked himself into the bathroom and wouldn't come out.

He kept telling me that he wasn't coming out the bathroom until I left but he knew I wasn't going nowhere so he stayed in the bathroom until I fell asleep then snuck out the house. I didn't realize he was gone until I woke up. I tried calling his phone but he wouldn't answer and hadn't returned home in a couple of days. A few days later he called me back to explain to me that he wasn't coming back until I left. He said he didn't feel safe sleeping at home while I was or am there. So basically he was saying our situation or relationship was over. I found out he cheated on me and went crazy on him so now I had to go. We planned the day I would have all my stuff packed for him to pick me up and drop me off wherever it was I was going. I ended up at my biological mother's house.

Looking For Love

By this time my biological mother had her own house. Renting a two bedroom duplex on the corner of Schoenher and East Seven Mile, directly behind the store. My mother had somewhat of a job and seemed to be thriving from the outside looking in. Once I was there, in the inside of things, would I be able to be things clearer and for what they really were. When I moved in as always I contributed to what I was told to contribute to. Nothing specific that I had to do on the regular basis besides take care of the kids, making sure they ate, made it to school, was picked up, homework and anything kid. I helped put food in the house and contributed money toward bills when asked. I celebrated my nineteenth birthday in this house. By this time I had gotten me a new boyfriend.

AB was almost the same height as me but a little taller so he was maybe five four in height. A hundred and seventy pound when wet. Barber by profession even though he had pretty good and long hair that came down to the middle of his back. He made his own hours and schedule. Whenever he wasn't at work we were together and when we weren't together he was at work. My daughter loved him and he played a great role in both of our eyes. We were together so much that he basically moved into the house on Schoenher. Contributing money to the household and whatever was asked of him as well.

Everything seemed to be going good. One day while over to my adopted mother's house visiting , my brother end up in a verbal altercation with a babymomma of one of our adopted mother's real sons. It went from just being words to the babymomma trying to knock my brother upside the head with a Franks Hot Sauce bottle. My brother did what he had to do to defend himself. Not to mention he was a child at the time and she way older than him. After the altercation my brother and I left our adopted mother's house to continue bout our day. Today was my brother's prom day. We made it over to our biological mother's house for my brother to continue getting himself together. Everything went off without there being a problem. He looked good as well as enjoyed himself for prom.

Now this brother whose babymomma it was, that belonged to our adopted mother was a little off to say the least. When he heard the story of what happened from his mother and his babymomma which were two different stories he chose to take the story of the babymomma and run with it. He was highly pissed that my brother had put his hands on his babymomma. It's okay for him, our adopted brother to beat, punch, smack his babymomma but not anyone else. My biological brother and I would have to deal with being chased in a car by this man all up and down East Seven Mile. He would jump out and chase us on foot or with his shot gun. We were young kids so we had that burst of energy to get ghost on people chasing us especially if they were old, we had somewhat of a head start. My brother ended up moving in with our biological mother as well.

Our adopted brother would end up catching my two biological brothers walking up East Seven Mile and Celestine. He would persue them on foot and catch the brother that assaulted his babymomma. He held my biological brother down so the babymomma could beat his knees in with the silver metal piece of the "Club" from the car. After the incident the ambulance would have to be called and my biological brother would be transported to the hospital to take care of his injuries. I would receive the phone call from my biological brother telling me of where he was and what had just transpired. He told me he was at St. John Hospital on Moross and Mack in Detroit, MI.

I wasn't that far away from the hospital when I got the phone call. I was on East Seven Mile and Hayes. I shot straight up to the hospital to check up on my brother. Once I had security in my mind that my brother was straight and okay I left to go over to my adopted mother's house to "Holla at" our adopted brother. When I left the hospital I rode through my old neighborhood of Saratoga to talk to one of my people about a piece. A gun. All this time I could have called myself gangster because in any incident or altercation I was willing to fight it out. Hands. No weapons but with this situation dealing with this grown man already armed I wanted to be armed as well. I was ready to kill this nigga for harming my brother.

 Take this nigga straight off the map, the earth as if he never existed. My connect was so gangster that when I whipped up on "Little G" he was like I'm riding. We called him "Little G" because he was short. Only like five feet maybe if he had on his gym shoes. The other reason was because he was so gangster and the neighborhood thug. Dark skin complexion. He put the chopper in the trunk of the car and we rode out. "Little G" also had two glock nines as well. By the time I made it to our adopted mother's house, her son had already packed up his babymomma, the baby, their things and left the scene. I pulled up acting all crazy.

Ready to go to war over my brother being hurt. Our adopted mother calmed me down. Told me that she understood my pain and where I was coming from but wouldn't tell me where her son had went. Our adopted mother did all she thought she could to calm the situation down but I was still upset. How could our adopted brother choose his babymomma over his family. That shit was crazy to understand. By the time my biological brother was discharged from the hospital he was officially moved in on Schoenher. We would wake up every day smoking weed. It was breakfast, lunch, dinner, dessert and in between snacks. With no problems of our own we lived care free.

One morning while living on Schoenher my brother and I woke to do our usual routine. I rolled the blunts as he washed his face and brushed his teeth. When we both were done getting ourselves together we went outside to the front porch to kick it so we wouldn't disturb the others still sleeping. While outside on the front porch doing our thing, our great-uncle pulled up. When he came upon the porch all he smelled of is alcohol. Liquor. It is every bit of only eight in the morning and he was already fucked up. Our great-uncle was drunk, babbling that drunk talk. My brother and I continued to pass our blunt back and forth as we laugh out loud at him. Shit got serious when our great-uncle walked up on me saying something to the sort of him getting fucked and sucked before he went back to work.

My sonar and impulses were going off crazy. I already had some what of an idea of what he was talking about and who it had come from. This was not my first time being approached or told these things. It had happened before with other people but not with family. I asked our great-uncle, "What did you say?" Our great-uncle repeated what he had just said. Said it twice to me I had now sobered up. I was shocked and disgusted by what our-great uncle had said and insinuated. Trash is what he is. Garbage that needed to be taken to the dump. I was adopted as a kid so I barely really knew any of my real biological family. Like know them know them. I didn't associate myself with any of them. I only spoke when I saw them. I knew nothing of these people and I didn't go by the things I over heard, was told and or assumed but after the talk I had with my granny I knew that this great-uncle was one of the people who molested my biological mother as a child. I always steered clear of him but now here he was in my face asking me if I could fuck him and suck him up before he go back to work.

I was astounded! Mouth on the floor. I wasn't a child anymore. Not easily intimidated or persuaded. I was nineteen and grown enough to make my own decisions and I wasn't going for that. I asked our great-uncle, "Where did he get his information from and how did he feel comfortable asking me some shit like that?" By this time, my brother and I were standing at attention with all eyes on our great-uncle. Ears big like Dumbo the Elephant we had them pitched out like tents. Ready to hear his response. Our great-uncle responded, "Your momma." I repeated, "My momma? What?" Our great-uncle began to explain what he was told, All the things he had heard. He started off, "I was talking to your

117

momma and she was telling me how you be out here tricking and fucking everybody for money." He continued, "Your momma told me you are a street walker, that you be hoeing. I thought I could come over here to get fucked and sucked before I go back to work. I got like twelve dollars if you want it."

My brother and I looked at each other as if we were thinking the same thing. Which we were but I didn't do it. My brother got to going the fuck off on our great-uncle. This brother and I are said to have the same parents. Both mother and father. We were both adopted and raised in the same household. We had a tighter bond then the rest of the siblings. He had been over six feet since the age of eleven. It was like he sprouted in his sleep and grew over night. So with my brother standing up he towers over any and all. Standing over our great-uncle my brother began to cut the rug. "What the fuck you talking about? My sister aint no hoe. She don't be doing none of that shit you talking about. Whoever told you that is a liar and you need to get the fuck on before I fuck you up." I appreciated my little big brother taking up for his big sister. That was mad love but I wanted to get to the bottom of this. I opened the front door and called out for our mother. She eventually came to the door asking what was going on.

When our mother came out onto the front porch she saw all three of us standing around looking crazy. I said to our great-uncle, " Tell her what you told us. Tell her what you just told me." Our great-uncle turned to our mother and repeated the same words that he had said in front of my brother and I to her. You could see the look change on her face from that early morning I just woke up to looking stupid. When the great-uncle was done our mother shouted, "I didn't tell you anything like that. I didn't say she was a street walker I said she be walking the streets. I didn't say she be fucking everybody I said she know everybody." She continued, I didn't say she was a hoe I said she know a lot of hoes." After she said that she started saying to our great-uncle, "Why would you bring that bullshit over here?" Our great-uncle replied, "Well you the one told me that she would trick with me. My bad for bringing this to your house. I'll leave now."

That left my brother and I standing on the front porch staring at our mother in disbelief. Who the fuck does or says stupid shit like that? All I could say was, "Wow!" Our mother wanted us, me to brush it off like it was nothing. Her defense was she really didn't say what our great-uncle said she had told him. I wasn't ready to let it go. Like I said before this wasn't the first time it had been said to me about tricking or having sex for money. A couple of my mother's male friends had approached me and said the same thing to me about tricking. Most of them, right after they had just got done doing whatever it is they do with her. I figured that's what they were doing with her.

The home being my biological mother's house, me being her child and living in her house she expected me to abide by her rules and up until that moment I was so respectful of all that but this time it wasn't going to fly. She had totally crossed the line. We verbally began to argue. The argument had got so intense that it came to her jumping in my face again telling me on how she was going to fuck me up like a "bitch in the street." So me being sarcastic said, "Well lets go outside," and proceeded outside. When I made it to the street my mother announced that she wasn't coming outside and she wanted me to take "that shit" away from her house. I told her that I wasn't going nowhere. She ended up calling the police on me.

The first time they came they didn't take no one but the second time they came the police arrested me for "making a disturbance." The police took me down to the Nineth Precint on Gratiot and Gunston. While I'm in jail trying to call people collect the police told me that they were just going to hold me for a couple of hours until they thought things had calmed down then they were going to release me. The police put me in a cell and left. When they returned the officers informed me that I had a warrant out for my arrest in Harper Woods for violation of probation. I was placed on probation for an event that had occurred at Eastland Mall on East Eight Mile Road and Vernier. Young and reckless I almost acted out in all places if it came down to it and the mall wasn't having it that day, I was sixteen when this happened.

The officers also informed me that they would be putting in a call to Harper Woods so they could do an inmate pick up. If Harper Woods chose not to pick me up the officers were going to still release me like they said they would. When the officers left from talking with me I immediately started praying to the "prison gods" and laid down on the cold concrete slab the jail had as a bed. No cover so I used my coat to put over me to keep me warm. Once I eased my mind a little I dozed off to eventually be woke up by an officer calling my last name. I saw a black male officer turn the corner I got excited because I was thinking that "Detroit" was going to let me go.

Up until I saw another male officer hit that same corner but he was white. I instantly knew that this white male officer was from Harper Woods. One being he was white and at this time all the majority of the white officers lived and worked out in the suburbs. Harper Woods would be a suburb of or around Detroit. Two was because he came alone. I mean even if I was a female like come on, it took two black officers to come pick me up in Detroit. Anyways back to the story so Detroit Police were now releasing me to Harper Woods Police and they were to transport me to their department. The ride was silent. I had nothing to say and didn't know what to say. A moment I was speechless or at a loss for words. In the back of the squad car I tackled my boxes of information that I had stored in my brain for anybody that I knew cared about my well-being enough to want to come bond me out. Later on for me to repay them.

I wrecked my brain for people I knew still had a land line phone because at this time you couldn't call cell phones collect. Only land lines. Then the person receiving the phone call had to choose to accept it or not. By this time it is the middle of the night. I ended up calling the older gentleman that I had met when I was sixteen. He came right to get me. No questions asked. I was home before daylight. Come to find out AB had camped out in his car all night waiting on me to call and say what my bail was. As we were pulling up I saw him laying back in his car so I had the older gentleman go round the block to drop me off. Before I got out the car I explained my situation to the older gentleman and he was understanding. I thanked him and told him how much I appreciated that he came through for me. Hugged him and proceeded to get out the car.

 As I was exiting the car the older gentleman said to me, "Just make sure you there when I call upon you as well."   I walked around the corner to the house and got into the car with my boyfriend. My boyfriend and I discussed the events that had occurred that day and everything that lead up to me being arrested. All he had to say to me was that I needed to apologize to my mother to try to smooth things over so I would have a place to stay until he got things situated for my daughter and I to come and stay with him so I did. A couple weeks after me being arrested I wake up one morning to find a note plastered to the screen door. I snatched it off and read it. At the top it read, "Notice of Eviction." Somewhere in the lines it also read that our mother was behind almost three thousand dollars in rent. She hadn't paid rent in almost four to five months. I grew confused. If our mother was not paying rent then what was she doing with the money we gave her for our half of the bills or rent.

   I woke up my little brother after me to let him read the paper as well. We both were disappointed. Not only had we been contributing to the bills but we were also taking care of the kids as well as the household. Our mother was always complaining about not having money for this and not having money for that so that is why we were thrown all the way off by the eviction. Another reason being that that we thought that we could trust her and believe what she told us. My little brother and I sat down to try to figure out what was happening and why it was happening. Eventually our biological mother would join us on the front porch of the house where I would hand her the note that was stuck to the screen door.

Our mother would flip the story from us getting evicted to me always being in her business, "Trying ," to be grown as she would say it. This time I would walk away from this situation knowing that our mother had it in her to call the police and have one of her own children sent to jail just to validate herself and make her feel as if she was in the right instead of the wrong as she always seemed to be. A few days after the eviction notice while little brother was in Mt.Clemons registering to attend classes at Baker's College. I was sitting under the dryer at Better Fashion's Hair Salon waiting to get my hair done I received a phone call from my mother alerting me that it was going down and that she needed me to get there. Where ever "there" was. I bolted from the chair and right up East Seven Mile from Hoover to Schoenher to find a crowd gathering in front of my mother's house. In the midst of the crowd were my mother and my siblings standing around their car being surrounded by the crowd that was forming. I was a born firecracker and a born fighter. It was another thing I enjoyed and loved to do.   I felt I was so good at it.

 When I ran up on the crowd I ran right through it to make it to my family to let them know that I was there. When I ran up I shouted the words, "What up," signaling to anybody who had the beef to bring it. Our next door neighbors was a dyke, gay or lesbian couple and he female that played or acted as the dude was the first to approach me talking shit. The dyke neighbor was telling me was kid and to stay in a childs place as she walked up on me. As the neighbor got closer to me my younger sister ran up on the side of her and told her to leave her sister alone. The female looked down toward her side and yelled get the fuck away from her to my younger sister. By the time the female stood back up straight to face me my fist was introducing itself to the whole right side of her face.

The impact of the punch was not expected by the crowd because after the impact the crowd gasped as they watched the dyke female fall to the concrete cement she was once standing upon.   Once the crowd heard and saw the impact of the punch, they began to disperse and go their separate ways. When the female finally came to, she picked herself up off the cement and tried to figure out where she was.   The female's girlfriend ran to her side to assist and aide her in her recovery.   Once it had settle in the female's head of what just had happened she became frustrated again and wanted to attack the duplex that we shared with them.   Threatening to bust out all windows if I didn't come out.

Once I came out the house the female changed it to burning the house down if we didn't leave.   At that moment it was planted that we had to go. Everything had come to a head with this incident and the eviction notice.   I took it as a sure sign that it was time to go.   My mother gave me the keys to her car so I could go view a couple of houses we had chose as potentials.   She packed the kids up in the car, gave me what I considered to be a wad of money with a hundred dollar bill on the outside of the roll and sent me on my way. I viewed the properties and chose the house that was available right then at that moment. It was a bungalow located on the Westside of Detroit off of Grand River and Livernois. When I went to exchange money with the landlord I pulled out the wad of money given to me by my mother to discover that it was only two hundred fifty dollars.

The amount needed to move in was nine hundred and fifty dollars. Once I discovered the amount that was given to me by my mother I decided myself not to give the landlord the move in cost. Not because we didn't have the money but because I had two times more than the amount requested. Who thought that they could move in with only two hundred and fifty dollars. My mother was tripping. I returned back to the duplex to inform our mother that I didn't find anything suitable and that we had to figure out a plan b. The plan B was to get a U-Haul truck and rent out a room until tomorrow morning when we could get back on the search for a house. We would relocate from Schoenher to move into the rooms at the Eastland Motel on Gratiot and Eight Mile. Double bedrooms were fifty five dollars and single rooms were thirty five dollars. My mother needed a double bedroom for the four kids and herself. I got the single room for my little brother, my daughter and I. Leaving my brother to camp out in the chair and or the floor because my daughter and I consumed the bed.

The next morning she would give me the keys to her car to continue viewing properties. As I saw it she wasn't serious about moving. She had no source of income and no other way to replace the money being spent daily. When I did have access to her car I would be I the streets hustling trying to double my profit. Whenever my mother left the room she would always say that she was headed to some money but always came back broke with no food for the kids or gas in her car. Seemed to me like she was out in the streets just to be out there with no productivity. After almost a month of being at the room I had began to become fed up with babysitting the kids while she ran the streets. I was tired of paying for her room while she laid around like everything was good. One morning our mother returned from her day/night and morning out with no money. She had left yesterday afternoon only to return minutes before check out time. My mother came down to my room which was in a different building on another side. She came down to talk to me to let me know that she didn't have the funds to pay for the room, food or gas. I politely explained to her that I couldn't keep paying for her room. It was cutting into my saved funds. I also explained to her that I could not get out to hustle for more money because I was always stuck in the room with the kids while she was in the street doing nothing to benefit us. We passed words back and forth between each other until she asked me to watch the kids while she made a run to pick up some money.

Which I did only for her to return several hours later to pick the kids up. When I walked the kids out to the car I spoke to her about what she was going to do. All she kept saying to me was that she was only concerned about her and her four kids. Anything and everybody else didn't matter to her then she pulled off leaving my little brother, my daughter and myself at the room. Months would pass. The weather would go from Fall to Winter. I would still call and try to contact our mother but to no avail. She wouldn't answer or return my phone calls so one day I decided to stop calling. For Thanksgiving we were invited to Granny"s house for dinner. We would leave right after our extended checkout time maybe like one in the afternoon to head to granny house. Once we were there to congregate with the family that showed up.

We would discover that our mother had finally gotten another house and a live in boyfriend. Once again I was confused to how our mother could leave us in the situation she had left us in because of her bad decisions. I couldn't understand why she hadn't tried to contact us or invite us to live with her before she invited her nigga. Once again I was stuck in the same place of misunderstanding that I once stood in as a child. Stuck once again in the same place. Still trying to put some type of explanation to the story or situation at hand to give our mother the benefit of the doubt. To try to give her some type of credit for the things that she lacked on the constant basis. Trying to give her credit for something she hadn't even done and or wouldn't do. I was trying. Even when she wasn't.

 I ended up calling our mother to wish them a happy holiday to make it seem as if it was out the blue. She answered and told us to come visit so we did. Thanksgiving night was spent at granny's house and the next morning to afternoon my little brother, my daughter and I caught the bus from Hazelwood and Linwood downtown to the connector bus to the eastside of Gratiot and Liberal Street. Arriving at the new house it was a standard from the outside. The inside was an average three bedroom with a living room. We would end up spending the whole day at the our mother's house. She would eventually ask us to come to stay with her. Offering us, my brother, my daughter and myself the basement.

After relocating all our belongings over to the house we got comfortable in the unfinished basement. As I laid upon the couch glancing up to the ceiling of the basement. I could see all the spiders, spider webs and cotton balls in every corner. When I got comfortable enough I feel asleep to be woken up by my little brother swatting a spider coming down from the ceiling getting ready to land on my face. I woke up going crazy. I am really scared of spiders and little crawling insects. They creep me out. With me making all that noise I guess I woke up the boyfriend and our mother. She came out her room and start going crazy. Yelling and being belligerent. Once told of the incident, our mother said that I could move upstairs but only to the kitchen. So the little nook in the kitchen where the kitchen table was supposed to go now lay my bed. I wasn't complaining because it was better than the basement. The situation and or relationship between our mother and I would not seem to get better.   We would occasionally get into yelling matches with each other and the only way to make the situation better was to give in to her requests and or just be nice to her.   Kissing of the ass as you would say.

Freaky Jason

While over in this neighborhood of Liberal between Monarch and Queen I would encounter new and old friends. One old friend would become a new friend in a new way. This man and I would have a ten year age difference between us. I had met him once before when I was fourteen years old. I was traveling from my adopted mother's house over to my biological mother's house by foot. Walking from Saratoga and Schoenher to Saratoga and Hayes. I encountered a group of men standing in the front yard of a house. All would look and glance upon the young mother walking her baby up the street in a baby stroller. Whistling and saying things aloud but only one would approach this young mother to find out that she was only fourteen. The man would apologize and rejoin the group of males in the yard. Only to be reacquainted five years later.

The relationship with my barber boyfriend never ended or we didn't break up as most would. It was just time for me to let go of him until I could get myself together first. Wasn't no point to me in having a boyfriend while I was living in a room. If anybody, any man wanted to be with me he would have made the situation better by helping me find and or offering me a place to stay in my time of need. With the situation of us living in a room I didn't have time to be focused on a boy or a man so I had no boyfriend. I was too focused on getting us up out that room. While walking up the block of Novara toward Gratiot on Detroit's Eastside headed to the store I would encounter this same man almost in the same circumstances.

It was a yard full of niggas but this time they were working on a house. This man approached me and introduced himself as "E" leaving me with his business card but I never called him. On another occasion I was walking around the corner of toward Hayes and he pulled up on me with his friend asking a thousand and one questions about why I didn't call him and what was the point in taking the number. Before he pulled off I had to promise him that I would call him that night or he would have followed me to where I was going. When I called "E" later that night, we ended up talking on the phone for almost four hours. We talked about almost everything. It was like we had already known each other. After that night "E" would be on my co-tail hard "grooming" me to become his girl as he would later say.

Calling me to check up on me. Seeing where I was, what I was doing even who I was with. One time "E" popped up at my biological mother's house without even calling trying to catch me in the "act." Sure enough these were the signs to show me that he was crazy but I didn't know exactly. Like really, I didn't know the full scale of his craziness. I thought that "E" was over-loving if that is even a word. He was crazy in love and wanted to keep as well as protect what he deemed was "his." Me being his girl and all. After the crazy popping up incident "E" asked me to move in with him. I agreed. My situation or relationship between my mother and I wasn't getting better. Amongst many other reasons I considered to be pros at the time. Plus, I wanted to show and prove to "E" that he had a good girl and that he could trust me.

The house that I met "E" working at on Novara and Gratiot would later turn out to be his own house that he was renovating and adding additions. This is where my daughter and I would relocate to. This house was three bedrooms. Two bedrooms downstairs across the hall from each other and the master bedroom upstairs. My daughter would end up with her own room and of course me upstairs in the master bedroom. The renovations that "E" made to the house was he added a fish tank in the middle of the wall, in the wall. New kitchen and bathroom with a Jacuzzi upstairs and downstairs in the basement. Amenties that I was not accustom to. Every day I, we were in the jacuzzi. "E" not only worked on houses and cars but he also was a man of the "streets." We had money every day to do whatever we wanted, whenever we wanted to do it. We brought what we wanted when we wanted to.

In this house we were living as we had never before. Not because we had not but because "E" taught me to do other things with my money like save. "E" was willing to pay for and buy everything so whatever couple dollars I did have I put to the side for those rainy days everybody talked about. That just in case money. Just in case of anything. Of course the stash would grow but not really prosper. Every other day I felt the need to help a family member out with this and or that. Loan them this and they will pay me back type shit but everybody know how that go. I felt that it would be selfish of me to hold on to something I knew somebody else needed. Whether it being money or anything of the sort. The way my life and situation was set up everything was good and taken care of so why not do a good deed and help the next person out. Especially family.

In the meantime and in between time I was still taking from myself not even knowing. After a few month of being with "E" he brought me a car. A ninety eight Pontiac Grand Am so I could come and go as I pleased without waiting on him. This car would be the start of some of our problems in our relationship. With me having the car I was up and out early every day running the streets. Spending money only to come home with bags and bags of clothes. One evening upon returning home I found "E" home. Which was unusual only because it was too early in the day for him to be home. I know, I know. Home too early? I know but back to the story. When I made it through the door I had arms as well as hands full of shopping bags. I found "E" standing in the dining room with a few of his homeboys discussing what I thought was business.

When I came through the threshold all the speaking tongues stopped. I spoke and continued my way on upstairs to the master bedroom to put my items away. "E" would come up after he walked his guest out. "E" would start off by telling me that someone tried to break in our house. Leading me downstairs to the bedroom window where the screen had been cut in an attempt to pry the window open to gain access to the house. Then

"E" would start to tell me that if I would have been home instead of the streets bullshitting. That whomever tried to break into the house only tried to break in because they knew I wasn't home. Yada, yada, yada. So forth and so on. So in my defense I tried to explain to him that I didn't know what was going on and that I would start being home more but the more I talked and accepted the blame for nothing in my control I grew angry and frustrated. I ended up telling him that I was not a prisoner of the house and that it was not my duty to protect it.

"E" and I would end up going back and forth in an argument until I decided we needed some time and space to ourselves. I left only to return around the corner to my biological mother's house. "E" and I didn't talk for days after I left. My pride was too high at that time so I decided that I wasn't going to be the one calling and begging to come back even though I didn't want to be in the same house as my biological mother. I had become accustom to living the good life stress and care free.

The situation and circumstances were the same at my biological mother's house. Every opportunity I had I was out the house to keep the drama down. During this time of our brief break up I was offered the opportunity to go travel and model in a competition in Atlanta, Georgia. Without a second thought or hesitating I accepted. Modeling was a hobby that I enjoyed very much. Another hustle of mine that I was more than interested in. I loved modeling with a passion.

Every chance I got I was volunteering myself to other stylist. The beautician I had been modeling for and working with was a man by the name of Mr. Little. Besides going out of town to Cedar Point with my eighth grade graduating class, my opportunities with Mr. Little took me out and away from the city and state the most. I enjoyed every minute of being out of city. From the different types of people to the difference in environment. Whenever offered the opportunity to get M.I.A. I took it. I didn't tell "E" that I was leaving. When "E" finally decided to call me I had been out of town for three days. When he found out he sounded angry and disappointed at the same time. Having me to promise him that when I made it back to Detroit I would call him to let him know that I was back in the city.   Upon arriving back to the "Motor City" I called "E" to let him know what time I would be arriving back at my biological mother's house and when I pulled up "E" was there. Sitting in his truck, parked right in front of the house.

I took my things into my mother's house and came back outside to talk to "E". He offered to take me to grab a bite to eat. I accepted. While we were out and about traveling around the city not actually going to a restaurant we pulled up at a car lot where "E" would purchase me a two thousand two white Ford Explorer. Paid for. Cash in hand, drove the truck right off the car lot. Of course this was part of "E's" making up process and I was going along with it. We ended up spending that night together.   I guess that making up session put us back on. The next morning things were if they had never changed. Back to regularly scheduled programming.   As if nothing had happened.   All was forgotten to never be spoke upon again. Things would go up and down.   Back and forth in the relationship between "E"and I until one day everything just broiled over.

A few weeks before this incident "E" and I had gotten into it.   To keep me from leaving the house and going over to my biological mother's house he had started staying the night out.   The day of the incident "E" had left the previous evening returning the following morning.   After dealing with him being gone these last past weeks I was feed up. When "E" entered the home he came in as if everything was cool and I let him have it.   From the front door to the living room.   To the bathroom into the kitchen on up into the master bedroom.   I followed "E" throughout the whole house telling him how I was feeling until I had let everything out. When I finished we ended up having sex and spending the rest of the day together doing so until later on that night.   I woke up to find out that "E" had left while I was asleep.   When "E" returned the next morning it was over I had had enough. I was done talking.

I had always threatened "E" with leaving him so when he came home I had already had started packing my stuff and some of it was sitting at the front door. "E" knew what it was when he entered the door. The arguing started and before I knew it I was storming out the door toward my Explorer. After I left "E" that time I didn't want to go back around to my biological mother's house so I ended up moving in with granny. I felt I needed the extra space between "E" and I so I didn't have to see him every day. Plus, I didn't know how I would react if I saw him with another female. To me it was the best choice. I moved from Detroit's Eastside to the Westside. Now I resided on Hazelwood and Linwood in the upper unit of a three bedroom flat. In this neighborhood I would encounter a different type of hustle by shooting dice. I was so good at it that it had become an everyday thing. Almost a way of life. Producing whatever I wanted for that summer.

Paying bills. Buying cars, clothes, shoes and whatever else we may have needed. Granny didn't like the fact that I was out in the streets shooting dice with the guys for her own personal reasons. I believe because she is this older, elderly GOD fearing lady whom attended church sanctimoniously. Every time the church congregated. Going to all the services from the beginning to the end of the day. Granny not only volunteered her services and time but mine as well as. She did not complain when that same money was being spent on her or in her household. One early morning that previous winter while taking my daughter to school I had an accident in my Ford Explorer on Detroit's Eastside in front of the cemetery on Gratiot between French Road and Conners. I was trying to avoid a passing car that seemed to be merging into my lane way too fast. It seemed as if the car would come in contact with my car. I swerved to avoid the collision and ended up riding on top of the curb as if to be straddling a mad bull until the truck had stopped. The car was positioned on top of the fire hydrant.

I had took out a couple of the electrical poles which took down wires of all the poles headed toward Conners. During the incident I glanced over at my daughter who was strapped in to see what I thought was terror in her eyes and on her face so I tried to hold it together. Not knowing the outcome of the situation I should have told my daughter that I loved her but instead something in the back of my mind told me to start praying to GOD. So I did. Eyes closed and everything I began to pray to GOD out loud. When the first tear fell from my eye the rocking of the truck came to a halt. I opened my eyes to notice that the truck had came to a complete stop. I looked up and thanked GOD. Said Amen. Grabbed my daughter to hug her and at that very moment I told her that I loved her. It seemed as if GOD had heard my prayer and in magnificient timing my prayers were answered. (Thank YOU GOD).

I looked around to observed that everything seemed to be okay. I proceeded to move the truck but it wouldn't budge. I went from drive to reverse and there was still no movement. I looked over to my driver side mirror to discover the cables and wires. I gave them a shove off the mirror. I decided to exit the truck to see why we were not moving. Upon exiting the car I stepped into a puddle of water but remind you that this is the winter time in Detroit Michigan. Everything is frozen so where was this fresh water coming from? I bent down to look up under the truck to find that the truck had landed upon the fire hydrant. At the very moment I discovered the fire hydrant I also realized where the water was coming from and that there may be live wires down around us. I grabbed my daughter and we left the car as it was. On top of that fire hydrant. I would later get billed by the City of Detroit for this incident. Now I needed a new car.

The time I was down and didn't have a car it kept me close to home. Where ever home was. Living with granny on the Westside without a car kept me off the Eastside. In those few weeks of me being close to home I would begin the gambling excursion with the neighborhood hustlers. Learning and mastering the game of Four, Five, Six and raking all the boys in the neighborhood that called themselves hustlers. Hitting some of them so bad that some had to borrow their money back just to re-up or get back on. I would take my winnings from the dice game to provide for the family as well as whatever was needed in the household. I even took the money and brought granny and I both a car. Granny got an Acura Legend and I got a Probe. Even though granny had her own car she would never end up driving it. First off it was a stick shift and granny nor I knew how to drive one. Secondly, she had an extra set of keys to my car. Able to come and go at will. During this time I would also meet the third man to become my boyfriend.

Everybody called him "Fats". He was tall. Maybe about six four or six five or so. Thin, lanky of a dark skin complexion with greenish gray eyes because he said that he has Glucoma. "Fats" came into my life and spoke life into me. Telling me what was possible and what I was capable of. He gave me the strength to reach far out from within my grasp. He was my ray of sunshine throughout the entire day but "Fats" was a straight street nigga. Through and through. He loved him some streets. Woke up to the and even slept in them sometimes. I'm married to my grind and my hustle but "Fats" is married to the streets. Granny knew it and said so but that didn't detour me away from him. Something in this struggle called life had brought us together and I wanted to figure out what the purpose of it was as I do in all my relationships in life. There must be a purpose. The few months of the summer of two thousand six had long gone, my birthday had passed. I was officially twenty years old and just getting ready for life again. When life itself threw me another curve ball.

Back At It

Granny had received news that she was approved for senior citizen housing and was to move in by November. I was happy for granny to have gotten the apartment but the timing was a gift and a curse. We were already two weeks into the month of October so to me it was bad timing. Bills had been paid, money had been spent, money had been splurged. Not including gas money and the money for the extra activities we participated in. I was pissed off but I knew I had to get over that part of the situation. I had to keep my mind focused on grinding to get my money up to relocate my daughter and myself once again.

All the while "Fats" was right there by my side. Rooting me on in the stands as the audience, on the sideline as the team, even coaching in some instances. "Fats" and I both loved to shoot dice and was very good at it. "Fats" favorite game was Craps and mine was Four, Five, Six. Depending on what game the opponents wanted to play choose determined who would participate between us. We didn't want to shoot against each other. We would end of breaking the block a few days in a row. A couple days after the few we would be moving into a one bedroom apartment on Detroit's Eastside on Pelkey and Parkgrove. The conditions of this building were despicable to say the least. The carpet had just been ripped up. The bare floor had not been swept nor mopped. They had just bombed or sprayed for roaches by the smell and the many dead carcasses from the roaches just lay about the house. I looked at those things as minor. All it would take is a little cleaning to get that together verses my daughter and I being out on the street homeless and having no where to go.

It felt good knowing that only I could disrupt my life at that moment. I was not handing out or giving the chance to anyone else. I felt that now I was in control and controlled the situation as long as the money kept coming in. Once settled in the apartment the bedroom belonged to my daughter and the front room served as another make shift bedroom with a pull out couch. The first few months went by with no hassles and or problems but then it seemed that things and people like "Fats" were getting complacent. Meaning they were becoming too comfortable. I had my brothers, family and friends over to the apartment almost everyday like it was the party house. Never bringing anything with but coming to devour everything and anything that they could. Food, snacks and even the extra stimulating activities that I partook in.

I begin to complain when I noticed the repeated process of things that seemed as if they were never to change. I spoke upon them so that they could be noticed by all around. Everybody coming over partying, snacking and eating food but no one is contributing. Everything was good as long as I sat by to let it continue with no words, but as soon as I opened my mouth to speak it was a problem. I was acting or seeming to be better than others. I didn't care because at the end of the day the extra people were taking what was provided out of my household. Which was there and provided for my daughter. The situation would continue to deteriate even the relationship with my once superstar and champ "Fats". Our relationship fell apart because of his love for the streets and my love for him. Neither of us "Fats" nor myself had a nine to five or were going to school. We were both depending on our hustles to get us by everyday and for some time it did work.

I was great at saving and budgeting money. I always kept a well enough amount of money just in case. The first time it would come in handy is when "Fats" messed up his people sack and had fucked up the money so "Fats" came to me to give him the difference and I did. The second time this happened he had promised his mother that he would give her some money for her birthday. Then he needed to send his kids out of state some funds. Every other day it was a different story to get some money from me until it became an everyday thing to where not only was "Fats" taking my money but he would also take my car. To be gone all day long only to return with no money at all. Not even the money that I had given him. Eventually I took it upon myself to speculate and assume what was going on. This started the turmoil in our relationship.

I wasn't willing to keep giving "Fats" money out my pocket or letting him drive my car. He would storm out with an attitude to be gone for days at a time. Now that I wasn't providing what "Fats" wanted he was barely home and having one of my younger brothers living with me put a lot of stress upon me. My younger brother decided to take on a job traveling across the United States and ended up in California.   Upon "Fats" return back to the apartment the things regarding my younger brother were already transpiring "Fats" took my car to drop my brother off at the Greyhound Station in Downtown Detroit on Howard and Third. When "Fats" returned back to the apartment, all his things were packed and waiting for him behind the door. After a brief discussion "Fats" grabbed what little things he had and left the apartment. After this apartment I would relocate to another apartment but it would be in greater conditions.

It was a two bedroom with hardwood floors throughout the apartment. Came with fridge and stove with everything included but electricity. Located on Calvert and Hamilton. At the time of residing in this apartment I would still be "kicking it" with "Fats." He would be there from time to time and even gained a key to the apartment when he began to contribute towards the rent. That would only last so long once again before "Fats" would slowly but surely fall back into his old ways and old habits. One month "Fats" was short on his half of the rent so I covered it. The next month "Fats" had no money for the rent, I covered it but when the process kept repeating itself and "Fats" was always looking to me to have it. I just started acting as if I didn't. When "Fats" was laid in the bed sleep wondering who was knocking at the door I let him answer it to find out that it was the landlord looking for the rent money and let him give all the supposedly reasons why we didn't have it.

I begin to plan my escape from this situation even if that meant that I had to go back to my granny, so that's what I did. Granny had been in her senior apartments for a good year and a half. Granny became friends with many residents and the overseer of the building. By me stopping by to visit or to check up on Granny I had become recognizable as well. In the senior assisted living place seniors were not allowed to have live in residents so I was barely there. Only coming to sleep, bathe and get dressed for work. This living with granny would only persist for four months. November until February when income taxes came out. An apartment was the first thing I spent my money on. Right down the street from granny on the other side of Fort Street and West Grand Blvd but further toward the water on the park side.

I signed a six month lease and paid my rent up for those six months in advance because the job I had as a sales representative for Olan Mills at Macy's working at Eastland Mall was seasonal. I lived everyday peacefully. I was two checks in the hold waiting for them to be released and I hustled everyday by doing hair, lashes or whatever so I had money put up. During that summer my biological mother ended up moving out of the state to Missouri, to where one of her younger sisters was living. My mother decided to come back but with no means of nothing for nobody. Meaning they had no funds for gas, no funds for food, not even funds for a home or where they were going to rest their head when they touched down. From my understanding it was a unplanned moved like they just woke up one morning in Missouri like we leaving right now in this very instance and heading back to Detroit. That is exactly how it seemed.

My aunt, my biological mother's sister even left her husband and her job to come back to Detroit. Now who does that? Anyways back to the story. Even with me now having a one bedroom apartment with only enough space for my daughter and myself. I went far out and beyond the call of duty to extend my home to my mother and my four younger siblings and I did. It would only last not even two weeks. Within the first week I had found a four bedroom house located in Southwest Detroit on Michigan and Twenty-eighth Street. Signed the six month lease agreement and paid the rent up months in advance. It was such a great deal to me. The rent for the apartment was four hundred twenty five dollars compared to the four hundred dollars I was being charged for the four bedroom house. Before I got the chance to say anything or surprise the family with the big move everything went haywire. I got into it with my fifteen year old sister about something so little as eyeliner. My little sister said to me, "Who am I to question her if her momma didn't say anything." I later said to my mother, "Why would I house a child I cannot talk to let alone ask a simple question?"

Our mother explained to me that I had to take the time to learn my younger siblings. That they had changed and were changing now that they were growing up. I responded to her statement saying, "Well they need to learn about me because I am not changing." By the end of the week, my mother and my younger siblings had moved out of my apartment. They couldn't bear to live in my house with my rules and the issues that I had with the kids. When my lease was up at the apartment I still ended up moving into the four bedroom house. It was already paid for in advance before the bullshit hit the fan and I wasn't going to deprive my daughter or myself of the opportunity for the chance to say that we lived in a four bedroom house just the two of us.

The situation between my mother, my younger siblings and myself happen before I had the chance to announce the good news. Once my mother found out she made a big deal about me trying to "stunt" on her as well as my siblings until I told my reasoning for obtaining the four bedroom house. Once I told the story people had the chance to look at it for what it was and brushed whatever my mother was talking about right on out their heads under the carpet. After the story was told to my mother she kind of forgave me for that moment in time. Things seemed to be going good. My daughter and I had our own house. I had a job and still continued to hustle. My somewhat of a relationship with my mother didn't seem to be tense so we were living in the good days or so I thought until my six month lease was up. I couldn't renew the lease. The housing program was getting ready to open up their housing program. I wouldn't qualify for the house because I was low income and didn't make enough money to support having a four bedroom house having only two occupants in the household.

Try, Try To Try Again

With me being in good standings at the time with my mother and with the extra source of income it would bring into the home my mother accepted my daughter and I into her home after we had moved out from our four bedroom home. Things were going okay for maybe a week or so. I could tell or feel that there was some type of tension in the house. I never addressed it. I didn't know or didn't understand where it was coming from but everything went haywire before my two weeks were even in. One afternoon I was in the kitchen making the family pancakes to have for lunch when I heard my little sisters outside arguing with some females.

Then one of my sisters yelled for me and said, "Oh these hoes want it." I dropped the spatula, ran to the door to check the status of my little sisters then ran to the bottom of the stairs to yell upstairs to our mother that the girls were about to fight. Afterwards I ran outside to the aid of my younger

163

siblings trying to figure out the details of the situation at hand. Come to find out the girls were arguing with other girls who were older than them by a year or two aging from fifteen to sixteen years old. The situation had come about because the older girls were accusing my little sisters of trying to talk to their boyfriends.

Now first off I don't play with other people children. I know I don't want nobody fucking with mine. Once I heard the ages of the girls I told them to go home to get an adult because at the end of the day that is where it is going to lead to anyways. The little girls get beat up and go home to their parents any concerned parent would want to know what happen and the details thereof. I think so. After speaking to the other girls I turned to look and speak to my little sisters as our mother finally came out to see what was going on. I told my little sisters to leave whomever these girls were talking about alone. Obviously the other girls cared about these boys enough to want to fight over them and plus there was no telling what part the guys really played off into all of this. The boys could have been and always seem to be playing sides by telling this person this and telling the other person something else.

I began explaining to my little sisters that they could be doing some much more with themselves then worrying about and playing with boys. Our mother rudely interrupted me by loud talking over me asking the girls, "Where them bitches at?" After our mother stepped out on the scene I quietly crept back into the house feeling that my job was done by keeping my little sisters from fighting. Eventually the two older girls returned with a parent to talk with our mother who was still loud talking about releasing her "two pitbulls" referring to my two younger sisters. The other parent explained that it wasn't so much about fighting that it was about respect and took her children with her and left.

Our mother returned from the middle of the street to continue her tyrant of what just had happened. Congratulating my sisters on being, "bad and showing them" as she said. Then somewhere in the conversation my name was brought up. Somewhere to the lines of, I be talking all that shit about fighting but was scared to fight. Now I am never scared and I have never been scared to fight. Somewhere in my atmosphere I smelled and odor and it was foul. I walked outside and said, " I don't fight kids." All at once everybody started yelling back at me. I turned and returned into the house to continue making pancakes. I could still hear our mother outside. Talking bad about me as if I didn't have ears to hear any or all the things she was saying about me. I didn't respond. I finished what I was originally doing which was cooking. Fed my daughter and we went to sleep as if nothing had happened. Like nothing was bothering us because it was true. There was nothing.

The next morning after the kids went off to school my mother thought that I was still asleep as she carried on a conversation on the phone. I was in the basement where all my things were located. Rummaging through my bags trying to find my daughter and myself some clothes to wear. During the rummaging I could hear my mother carrying on a conversation with someone on the phone telling this person what she thought of me, what type of person she thought I was, how I was a hoe and needed her. How I couldn't take care of myself as well as my daughter so forth and so on. At some point I got frustrated and returned upstairs to the living room couch. I turned the television as well as the radio off. There was nothing but complete and total silence. When my mother exited her room I was the first thing\person she saw. She ended the conversation she was having on the phone with a, "I'll call you back."

She opened her mouth to speak good morning and I straight went in for the jugular saying, "If you have anything you want to say to me say it to me. If you have anything you want to say about me say that to me as well. Don't talk about me behind my back like I can't hear you or like I'm supposed to sit around here like everything is cool and it's not." I don't know how my mother felt when I approached her in the manner I did but I do know that she told me, "If you feel some type of way about what I'm saying about you then you know what to do." I responded and said, "Hell yes I do because you are lying" and the arguing started from there. The argument became so intense that I eventually told her that, "if it came down to it I would beat her ass in her own house if she choose to continue disrespecting me." All my mother kept saying was, "Get the fuck out of her house."

I began to pack my things as I called one of my friends to come help me relocate. As I did that my mother began to call around to different folks in the family to tell them of what was going on and how, "I'm the devil's child. Demon possessed and disrespectful." Before I could finish loading the truck my aunt was calling me telling me what she had heard. That I was welcome over to her house if I needed a place to stay. This is where I ended up after this spat with my mother. Now the terms of the situation at my aunt's house were the same as far as taking care of myself and contributing to the household. The situation was totally different.

The type of relationship we had was none so we began to build one. Laying the foundation. Piece by piece. Brick by brick. My aunt had lived out of town the majority of my teen to adulthood so we barely knew each other. We only knew what we had heard or what we were told by other folks in the family.

When I moved into my aunt's house, my other aunt that I had previously lived with also was living there. Upstairs with her three boys. My aunt had eight children and was pregnant with her ninth but only six kids lived with her. With myself and my daughter it was a very full house but my aunt made the room for us and we felt very much welcomed. My daughter and I got a room on the main floor of a three bedroom house. My aunt moved her room into the living room to give us her space. A few months after I moved in my other aunt moved out so I relocated upstairs to gain more space and to give back more space since I knew the baby was coming. After my aunt had her baby boy she would try talking with my mother about our situation and relationship with me but it always failed. Meaning it never had any good intentions on working out. It never did.

My aunt had the chance to see and hear how my mother really felt and what she thought about me. Which of course was not good but it wasn't my fault that my mother harbored jealously, envy and even malice for me. Toward me for some very important reason in her mind. In my mother's mind her reasoning was legit. Nevertheless, people always tried to help in the building or bonding of the relationship between my mother and myself but it never worked out. My aunt tried at a few times. All turned out worse than what they began. Eventually my aunt gave up, knowing she had more important things and people to be concerned about like herself, her own family and kids along with her new bundle of joy.

Before the newborn baby was a year old my aunt was approved for housing. She relocated from Detroit's Eastside all the way over to Detroit's Westside. Joy Road and Evergreen area, to a four bedroom townhouse.   In the midst of her leaving, I stayed and kept the house for my daughter and I so we wouldnt have to look for another one.   With a little time, sweat, blood, tears and money I renovated the house into a living quarter.   The whole house was basically redone.   From the walls to the bathroom.   The kitchen cabinets to plumbing and piping.   Repainted and refurnished to became the living space that it is today.

Outro

In the moments of this paragraph I still reside in this three bedroom house along with my daughter. My younger brother whom had moved out of state came back almost two years ago to live with me and within those two years he has registered for school, attended school, graduated and became licensed in his field of study.   He works fifty six hours work weeks making twenty five dollars a hour.   My brother had also moved out to get his own place somewhere so far as Twenty-Two Mile and Hall Road with his soon to be wife that he proposed to on Mother's Day of Twenty fifteen.   I've had the house in my possession for almost five years. During this time, I've had a lot or more than enough time to re-evaluate myself as well as my life and those around me.   I've come to the conclusion that I play apart in a lot of the mischief that was going on by simply partaking and participating.   I came up with and started demonstrating my newest train of thought which is, "Why be around people who you know don't make you good?" People who don't help you when you need it but expect you to come running to catch them before they fall.

I choose in my mind first and it slowly but surely crept its idealogy into my life. It applies to all. Family as well as friends. I cannot and won't deal with people or folks who ask something of me but cannot give or return the favor. I truly practice the do unto others as you would want done unto yourself. I may help out and turn my cheek sometimes but there is only so many times I can do that before I began to feel taken advantage of. The kindness for weakness thing. It is only so much a person can take before they snap, crackle and pop somebody across the face or head. To keep myself from reaching that point I stay to myself and choose who I deal with accordingly. I don't sit up around or hang out with nobody. I feel that there is no one in, around or even on my level. Mentally then so forth and so on.

There is no other person who sees every moment in every second of every minute of every hour of every day as a chance to upgrade, enhance and or elevate themselves. Mentally, physically and or emotionally. There is not no other person who sees themselves as the conductors of the train that they are riding on headed in whatever direction they are going. There is not another person in this world who can take full acceptance of how and why their life is the way it is or ended up the way it is. People are so quick to point the finger and blame others for self faults.

Im happier than I've been in recent years only because I found happiness within myself. I just graduated cosmetology school in March of Twenty-fifteen and open my own Clothing Boutique . I've been running my Home Healthcare business for ten years now along with the music, modeling, hosting, promoting, marketing and other miscellaneous things I have ventured off into.

Salutations

This book is called the Chapter that changed my life because at the point where I became pregnant I stopped existing as a girl who was a daughter and started living as a young lady who was a daughter but would eventually become a mother herself. The same person I was trying to build a relationship with and was supposed to be able to look up to I was becoming one. A MOTHER. At that point my life changed. I had to become something I had never seen with my own eyes. Something I had always heard about but never knew it existed in the flesh. I had to become the example to lead by and over these past couple of years I believe I have done so. I took the focus off of others to regain focus of myself and all the things I have control over.

Like the Serenity Prayer I no longer dwell over things out of my control and or what others do. I am only in control of me and what is in my rem. With my upbringing, my role model of a Woman, church and with my understanding of the Bible I'm mastering the craft of being human but following GOD.   First understanding is to understand. Second is to practice what you understand.   So the Bible teaches us that GOD made us in HIS image who is Alpha and Omega.   Perfect and whole. Wanting and needing nothing.   So if I am made in GOD's image, I am GODly.   From the time of my birth I was made perfect and whole.   Alpha and Omega.   Beginning to end.   Wanting and or needing nothing of this world because I was already born with it.